DI035930

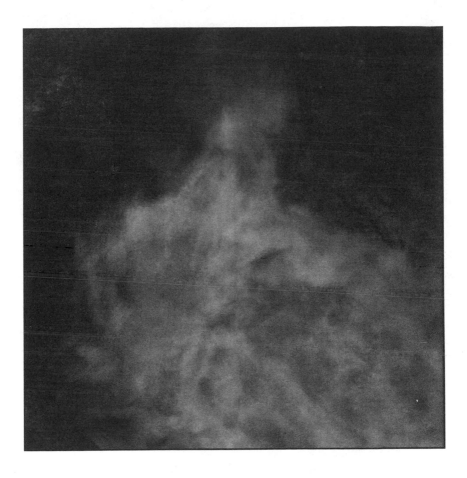

FALL ASLEEP FORGETTING

GEORGEANN PACKARD

THE PERMANENT PRESS • SAG HARBOR, NEW YORK

COPYRIGHT © 2010 BY GEORGEANN PACKARD.
ALL RIGHTS RESERVED.
PRINTED IN THE UNITED STATES OF AMERICA.

The author is most grateful to Julie Amper, Judith Shepard, and Joslyn Pine
for their editorial brilliance.

For permission to reprint material,
grateful acknowledgment is made to:

The lines from "maggie and milly and molly and may". Copyright © 1956, 1984, 1991 by the
Trustees for the E. E. Cummings Trust, from COMPLETE POEMS: 1904–1962 by E. E. Cummings,
edited by George J. Firmage. Used by permission of Liveright Publishing Corporation.

BOOK DESIGN AND PHOTOGRAPHY BY GEORGEANN PACKARD

This is a work of fiction. Names, characters, places, and incidents are either prod-
ucts of the author's imagination or are used fictitiously. No reference to any actual
person, business, company, or locale is intended or should be inferred.

All rights reserved. No part of this publication, or parts thereof, may be reproduced
in any form, except for the inclusion of brief quotes in a review, without the written permission of the publisher.

Library of Congress Cataloging-in-Publication Data
Packard, Georgeann.

Fall asleep forgetting / Georgeann Packard.
p. cm.

ISBN 978-1-57962-202-2 (alk. paper)
I. Title.
PS3616.A329F35 2010
813'.6--dc22
2010016929

For further information, contact
THE PERMANENT PRESS
4170 Noyac Road
Sag Harbor, New York 11963
www.thepermanentpress.com

FOR MY LOVING FATHER, DON,
A FINE JOURNALIST AND HUMORIST

AND FOR DIANNE,
WHO HANDED ME THE NOTEBOOK
AS I BOARDED THE TRAIN

AND FOR MY DARLING DAUGHTER,
RIVA

A day of mayhem
a moment of bliss
no matter
each night we lie in comfort and warmth
bedded down by gravity
teased into the earth and into a seductive semideath
a blanket of leaves falling gently on our faces
obscuring our vision bit by carbon bit
adrift we go
in acquiescence or defiance
no matter
as we fall asleep forgetting
the day.
And in the morning
with shining faces proclaim
that we are reborn
bathed in infant optimism
and the remembered fragments
of a dream.

SEPTEMBER 1959

She sits up straight in bed. The seasons have changed overnight; she can feel it in her bones. Summer has passed and the heady weight of a northern Michigan autumn is upon her, as sure as the musty dust of oak leaves that will follow.

From where she sits, back hard against the massive oak headboard, Fada can see deep into the orchard to the east. How she will miss these orchards with their intoxicating sweet fragrance of fallen apples, plump with rot. And she will surely miss the glorious morning light as it shoots low through the rows of apple trees, especially when it hits hard upon her Golden Delicious. The light transforms those trees into galaxies of yellow, bobbing suns. Then there is Crystal Lake, a mere ten-minute drive away; how she will long for its cold, honest waters.

But no matter. Yesterday, at forty-six, she had felt like an old woman. Today, she does not.

Fada's fingers graze the old quilt her mother had fashioned as a young wife. It must come with her, of course. Something about the hand-stitching and the geometric perfection gives Fada a sense of hope and order in the world. It has always graced her bed, even in the summer months. She rises and begins to fold the quilt lovingly, but then stops. She laughs at her sentimental attachment to this thing, as though it had life, as though it could love her back. *Will it comfort her in this new life she's chosen?*

The farmhouse is chilly and she dresses quickly in the clothes she'd placed on the cedar chest the night before. Her husband had left an hour ago. A doctor's day begins early and ends late, he has told her too many times. Of course, that had made his distractions and his infidelities easier to secret away. He has been an adequate husband and a father to their two sons only in monetary terms, always being so remote and self-important in his busyness. The thankless, everyday chores and the emotional clutter of family life had been hers to handle. But no matter, she concludes. She does not hate him. What she feels for him now is too small to be formed into anything as grand as hatred. Both her sons are now in Detroit, at university there. Her servitude, though having been lovingly rendered, is to them complete as of today.

"I'm not old," she announces with great conviction, "only my life is."

She puts on the percolator, cuts the wheat bread for toast, and then walks out into the east orchard one last time. This land, she knows, how it looks, how it smells, how it creeps into your bones so that you cannot distinguish between the cold of the earth and the cold as dense as ice in your bone marrow... *how can she live anywhere else after these twenty-five years here?*

She plucks a few perfect apples and stuffs them into the pockets of her overalls. He detests these overalls—they had been his—and prefers to see her in simple cotton dresses. Those dresses will all be staying.

What will become of the rest of these apples, she wonders. Who will arrange for the picking and the hauling, set the selling price? Who will determine the variety and portion to be set aside for the cider press? "No matter to me," Fada says out loud. "Breakfast is waiting and there is much to be done before the sun sets."

Soon, she is ladling skimmed cream into her coffee, spooning her own whole-berry strawberry jam onto the toast. She takes her well-measured time and relishes her lightheadedness. Everything feels as if she is doing it, tasting it, for both the first time and the very last.

Most of what she will need has been packed for weeks and stored in the root cellar, a place he never visits. Never would he have looked into her empty drawers or noticed the missing cookware, utensils, even the tools, which only she uses. Boxes of canned tomatoes, jams, and pickles are all neatly stacked with the potatoes and carrots. There are a dozen or so books boxed, including a book on modern painting that her hands have travelled over page by page many times. She favors nonfiction, and had added books on carpentry, gardening, and a single cookbook. A few family photographs, a sun bonnet, a radio, her address book, the leftover cash she has been squirreling away in a red, rusted-metal toolbox for years. *Years!* Only $357 are left, but it will buy the gas she needs to reach Fort Meyers and must hold her until she finds employment. Fada knows that she can live contentedly on very little. Farm life makes a person strong, efficient, frugal.

She begins to load the '51 Ford pick-up. This is her vehicle; he finds it too common, too coarse, and prefers his bloated Packard. She finishes the loading with room to spare.

Fada makes their bed, but takes her feather pillow. She pulls the two letters to her sons from her underwear drawer. In them, she details her plan, but not her destination, her love, but not her lifelong devotion. It will be awhile before they hear from her. They are not to worry— she is a capable woman.

Last week, she had purchased for the asking price, paying in cash, a 1954 Flying Cloud. It was a twenty-two-foot Airstream trailer, a thing of great beauty and practicality in her eyes. She had bought it from a man whose wife had recently died. The husband and wife had traveled to Nevada with the trailer twice, had even lived for a winter in it. He hadn't the heart to keep it after she'd died, and had placed an advertisement of sale in the paper.

Fada had a dear and widowed friend in Traverse City, Charlotte Hastings, who agreed to store the trailer in her barn. The previous owner had delivered the Airstream there for her, and Fada had arranged for a hitch to be put on her truck. She then kept the truck backed up to the chicken coop and hoped her husband would not grow suspicious. If he had noticed, he had never questioned her. It all seemed too easy, but then, of course, a husband's indifference can sometimes be an asset.

By late afternoon on that perfect September day, with an apple clutched between her teeth, Fada feels a pleasant dizziness as she drives southeast along State Road 115, away from Beulah and every habit that had defined her life thus far.

She will spend the rest of her days in Florida in the company of like-minded friends. Near her life's conclusion, she will bequeath all her belongings to a granddaughter she has never met; but based on her son's descriptions in his infrequent letters, she reminds her very much of herself. Stoic, intensely private, a bit odd.

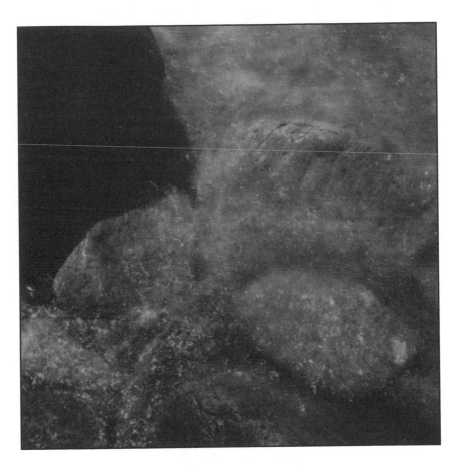

MAY 2001

THE LIGHT, THE ELEMENTS, THE MOVEMENT...
THEY ARE THE MESSAGE.
I AM MERELY THE MESSENGER.

LIES ABOUT THE BEAUTY OF SUFFERING

It had taken the Long Island Railroad thirty-nine minutes to deliver Paul Lang from Greenport, the railroad's easternmost terminal on the North Fork, to Riverhead, where Flanders Bay meets the Peconic River.

There Paul meets with a lawyer, a woman who seems to him barely old enough to have finished high school. Paul tells her that he needs a will—not a complicated matter, what remains of his life after death will go to his wife. Then he explains that his real problem is his life insurance and the ramifications of a less-than-accidental death. He has the policy with him. Paul is very straightforward. The lawyer is very uncomfortable.

She advises that, if allowed to, he should cash in his policy, and make some investments for his wife. She is not a financial adviser, she admits, but can recommend one. She reminds him before he leaves her shabby little office that what he plans to do is illegal and, consequently, she will be destroying her notes from this meeting. She refuses his check and wishes him well.

Paul finds a luncheonette on Main Street and Roanoke Avenue, eats some soup, and then hurries with his hand inside his belt to the bathroom behind the kitchen. Then he sits for a bit at the counter, sipping weak tea, killing some time until the 4:23. Later, as he walks along the Peconic River, he is assaulted by the dense, oily aroma from a McDonald's on the other side and vomits into his *Suffolk Times*.

Without consulting his watch even once, he arrives at the station just as the train approaches. Paul sits on the upper tier of the double-decker diesel, already bone cold. Why, he wonders, do they crank up the air-conditioning so. He brings his legs up to his torso, pressing his toes into the molded plastic of the seat in front of him.

Once heading east, the train makes an unannounced stop at the edge of town and sits there. The pain in Paul's abdomen is radiating in circular lurches to his back. He turns and stares out the window. A dilapidated concrete building sits in an empty corner lot. Weeds poke through the cracked parking lot, and sickly cedars and dead deciduous trees guard the property lines. The windows of the one-story structure—*had it been an auto repair shop?*—are all boarded up with irregular pieces of plywood and the wounded roof sags. Broken glass and trash litter the slab of pavement. Shreds of plastic bags impaled in the trees flap like flags of surrender. Nothing is alive or of any use.

"Could this day be even one shade bleaker?" Paul says to the empty seat beside him.

He thinks about the long months it took for his own father to die. He closes his eyes and sees that room, ironically the living room, in his grandmother's house. There his father is enthroned upon his hospital bed, bitter and resplendent in his foolish bravery. Yes, he is the king of death, removing his oxygen mask to say, "I will beat this thing. You watch me." And they all do watch—they see the stained sheets and his bloody spit in a metal pan, and the way his brown skin creases like eroding bluffs around his lips. And they witness the closing in of the flocked wallpaper and his pathetic smoking until he can no longer breathe on his own.

Paul had been only eight. He had hated his father for his dying and had hated himself for feeling that way.

The train begins to crawl forward and once they have just passed the hideous building he looks back to see a vine vigorously invading the eastern side and back of the structure. It is a wisteria, heavy with lavender blooms, growing outside, inside, and out the top of the roof, and even falling to cover the pavement beneath it. The vine seems to Paul to spread its arms in all directions, caressing the decrepit structure as a child might lovingly trace the wrinkles in his grandfather's face.

The scent of blooms comes to Paul…not from outside but from his memory, from that house where his father had died, from where that vine had grown unattended over the garage just outside the living room window, in Hamtrammack, in another lifetime.

Sometimes, he thinks, there is great pain in witnessing beauty, and perhaps great beauty in pain. "I don't know," he says out loud, and then hands his ticket to the bewildered conductor who appears before him.

"I'm sorry about the delay," the man says. "Nothing we could do anything about, you know, debris on the tracks."

Paul smiles. "And a lot of it."

And he decides right then that he will cash in the insurance policy and pay off the beach house. Sloan will have that, at least, and the restaurant to keep her occupied. And the box of poems.

Once the train is again swaying side to side heading eastward, Paul's thoughts are still focused on his wife; this keeps his mind diverted from the persistent pain in his gut. *Can she survive his death?*

This thought leads him, while passing through Aquebogue, to the brutal tale of her brother's death. He had not witnessed it, but Sloan had blurted it out years after they were married, in a drunken barrage of disjointed nouns and verbs.

And then until the train clears Jamesport, Paul travels back to 1974 and to Prudenville, in northern Michigan. Sloan is only six and Richard—brash, tall, lean Richard with his long hair bleached nearly white by late summer—is a mighty fourteen. Being beautiful yet introverted, Sloan finds in her brother her link to life itself, or at least this is how Paul imagines she feels.

As a boy, Paul had once been to Prudenville for a weeklong vacation with a white friend's family. His dark skin was an oddity; he had seen not one other like him the entire week. He had loved Houghton Lake. Poised at the lip of the village, it was a large and embracive body of water, shallow and safe for such a long distance from shore. He had learned to swim there and fished, even on rainy days.

The family had rented one of the many cottages that lined the narrow streets of Prudenville. He recalls easily the linoleum floors, the stained feather pillows, and mismatched plates and silverware. There had been a hot water heater proudly visible in the bathroom and bunk beds with lumpy mattresses. All a magical change from the harsh realities of Hamtrammack. And he remembers, as well, the strange children who lived year round in this fantasy world. He thinks of those blonde children with faces tanned nearly as dark as his, children like Sloan who every year endured the unyielding winter winds off the lake and the long wait for summer.

The train has nearly made Southold station when Paul gets to the meat of his memory. He embellishes it with the adjectives, adverbs, metaphors, and all the prosodic mush the poet utilizes to transform pain into beauty, or chaos into meaning. He visualizes things he has never seen about the town and its people, things like swims after dark without suits, and town drunks to be avoided, and musty movie houses where a city boy might take advantage of a local girl. But then Paul returns to the little he does know.

On one particular late-August afternoon, perhaps an hour before suppertime, Richard and two of his friends venture out in an aluminum rowboat with a small girl, sweet Sloan, wearing a dirty, orange life jacket riding up under her chin. Her brother rows on and on out into the lake, drunk on the pull of the oars, a little further than they should be.

It is exactly like this, Paul thinks, or else something very similar. And now as the train reaches the point where Mill Creek meets the southern edge of Hashamomuck Pond, he squints to see instead the silken surface of Houghton Lake.

Something like this does happen. They stop and anchor the boat, and the boys throw their bodies over the sides. Sloan watches from the boat and, at first, their antics frighten her, but then she relaxes and smiles. It is only Rescue, a game they often play. One boy jumps overboard and feigns drowning using melodramatic, desperate gesturing, pretending to be the pale-skinned cottage renter. The other two will be the heroic local boys, fearlessly to the rescue.

When it is Richard's turn, his silliness makes Sloan feel like the more grown-up of the two. As his pleas become more exaggerated, more agitated and anxious, the others laugh all the harder, safe in the boat some thirty feet away. He is always the best, they all agree, the most convincing. His two best friends clutch the sides of the boat as their rubbery legs dangle uselessly in the water; they are laughing that hard. Then Richard disappears once again beneath the surface, and doesn't reappear—for too long a time. Next comes a horrible silence. They all stare at the spot in the water where he surely must reappear. Anything beyond that thought is unimaginable.

Then Sloan shrieks out her brother's name. The bodies of the two boys jerk into sudden action and they jump clumsily into the water. They swim to where Richard had been. Sloan throws herself into the water, and one boy swims back over to her, and the other dives down again and again in search of Richard. Soon both boys and the girl are crying and screaming until a large woman in a flannel shirt finally arrives in a powerboat. She pulls the limp, now silent girl into her boat, then dives into the water fully dressed.

With the eyes of the poet that he is, Paul visualizes this one final image. With the ephemeral beauty and speed of a bass leaping above the water's surface, a flash in foreign air, Richard's perfect life is both brief and over.

The train now is dissecting the neighborhoods of Greenport and approaching the final stop with noisy, diesel fanfare. Paul finds a *New York Times* on the seat in front of his. He then goes to his car and sits and reads the editorials, just to free his overindulgent imagination from Prudenville and Riverhead, and all those adjectives and images and lies about the beauty of suffering.

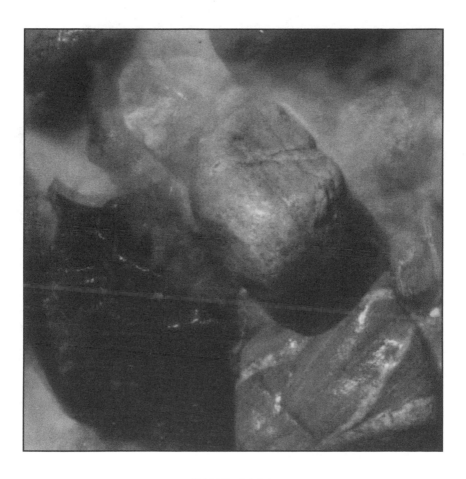

JUNE 2001

I AM ALONE ONLY TO THE DEGREE
THAT I SEPARATE MYSELF FROM THE NATURAL WORLD.

VOYEURISTIC GULLS

The North Fork has the heady ocean at its eastern tip, with bays and the Long Island Sound delineating both sides of this lovely, curvaceous body of land. There are expanses of vineyards and sweet little farm stands with hand-painted signs. This land is blessed with clear skies and seasons of equal length. Seems impossible to believe that a city of eight million is only 100 miles away. Here, even with the summer infestation of those city dwellers from the west, the miles of beaches are usually quiet and often empty.

As it is at East Marion County Park on this flawless June morning. The park is on the Main Road, State Road 25 (the only road heading east, between East Marion and Orient). It's a modest public beach and preserve that wraps around a creek off Orient Harbor to the south, and reaches to the massive Long Island Sound to the north. East of Dam Pond but just shy of Terry Point, it's a spot only a few people come to, mostly clammers, fishermen, picnicking families, or lovers on a day off.

But here this morning, like a flat, Mylar balloon, lies a body on the beach, deflated and limp. No one seems to know him, not Claude who discovers him, not the police officer she telephones, not the small crowd of people who later assemble to marvel at the corpse.

This woman Claude is a county employee who works six months a year, May through Halloween, here at the park, maintaining its structures and tending its beaches. She has already cleaned up most of the mess of winter—raking, pruning, removing fallen branches, laying more gravel in the parking field.

At the entrance to the parking field just a stone's throw from the body sits her eight-by-eight-foot fee booth, covered simply with rough-hewn planking. Last November, Claude replaced the asphalt shingles with a tin roof, not because it was in disrepair, but to increase the percussive sounds of rain. Inside the booth is a simple wooden desk where the phone she used to call the police sits. There is also a chair, pine wall shelving for park literature and seasonal permits, a worn rag rug, and three naked windows. Also on her desk is a gray, locking cash box, blank paper, a soup can filled with pencils and pens, a box of photographs, various books on horticulture and carpentry, and a first aid kit in a white metal box emblazoned with a bold red cross. The contents are old but adequate, the scissors slightly rusted and the delicate tissue around the gauze yellowed. She will not need these today.

Claude is the only park employee and arrives early each morning by bicycle from the trailer park where she lives. This makes her the logical person to come across what she assumes is his car, abandoned in the parking lot, the front tires in the sand and the driver's door hanging open. In the glove box the police will find a New York motor vehicle registration naming a Max Wretz of Flushing, New York.

It is Claude's responsibility to clean the long stretch of Sound beach, although this is the first dead body that needs removing. Sometimes she salvages usable wood that's come ashore and gives it to her carpenter friend, Barton. She once found a kayak, half-buried in the sand but in decent condition. She's waiting for a paddle.

Now she waits for the police to arrive. Cars pass, the sun inches higher. Later, she thinks, she will put out the wire-mesh litter barrels, repair a picnic table, and weed and mulch with pine needles the berry patches and perennial flowerbeds.

Claude is paid fairly for her work and it is the only income she has. Her personal expenses are modest—rent for her trailer slip, food, photographic supplies, and her lab usage fees in Riverhead. She has no car of her own, pays no insurance of any kind, and selects her wardrobe from the racks at the Opportunity Shop in Greenport. She cuts her own hair and listens to her radio or reads for entertainment. She has more money than she knows what to do with. Last year, she asked the county for less compensation; they thought she was kidding.

Claude now examines the body while she waits. He lies there on his left side facing the water, dressed in a white shirt and black slacks, shoeless. His legs are crossed and his white hair fluffs in the breeze like the feathers of the gulls who stand nearby, enthralled with the carrion.

She knows his being there will make everyone else's day feel unique. Thoughts about mortality will surface and inappropriate jokes will be made at the Blue Light. This is the first day of June. This is something to talk about.

The police and then the county detective arrive. They announce that he is dead and the crowd grows. The authorities take photographs, examine the sand, write down a few names and numbers. Then they take away the supposed Mr. Wretz in a minivan, and the winds and water soon erase his presence on the beach. And all those strangers who had seen his oddly seductive final pose will soon forget him as well. Except for Claude.

June 2

Can't get the picture of the body on the beach erased from that small screen at the back of my mind. I was hoping sleep would dull the image of sad, sad Mr. Wretz. But here he is still, as abandoned as his blue Plymouth. Strange how the car looked so hastily parked, as though he was dashing off to die. What brought him here?

On first waking, the mischief in dreams seems real and what is real, only dreamlike. Like that lost feeling I get when leaving a movie theater in daylight. Quickly enough, dreams fly from memory, scene by scene: The details are blurred as they dash to the subconscious. All I'm left with is...I can't fly. I'm not naked in public. I couldn't be attracted to her.

Then a certain object or person in the course of the day will jar free a fragment of a dream. I get a little jolt of fear or affection without understanding why.

Last night's dreaming leaves me with only an anxious feeling and a single image, blood seeping into sand.

After meeting Mr. Wretz, I ran along the shore, hard out without destination, in my bare feet. The coarse sand and little stones and broken tails of horseshoe crabs burnished the pads of my feet down to a new, raw layer. Once I'd stopped and was resting against a boulder, I noticed a broken line of blood, blood from my delicate winter feet, soaked into the sand like just another mineral. That blood in the sand, that image was in my last dream before waking.

So goodbye, Mr. Wretz. I imagine I'll see you too in my dreams.

HOLY TRINITY POKER

Many who live or summer in Orient are aghast at the thought of something so common as a trailer park here, not to mention one run by a transvestite. Their village is quaint, absolutely constipated with historic lore and architecture. There is even a slave cemetery. Trailer parks are for Riverhead, they wish they could say. But Cherry Grove has been here long enough to predate conventional preferences and historical society mandates.

It wasn't always called Cherry Grove. When Zygmont and Lucia Kazmierczak bought these two-plus acres back in 1965, the land was cheap, even though it bordered the bluffs of the Sound. They took out a loan on the land and the deluxe, two-bedroom mobile home that would occupy the first of the ten slips in the trailer park. Lucia, without much imagination, bestowed on the trailer park its initial name, Paradise Grove.

The land dangled at the end of a flimsy dirt drive called Roberts Road. There was a simple woodworker's shed and plenty of deer and fox, stubby black pines, cedars, oaks, and brambles. Zygmont spared as many mature trees as he could when he selectively cleared the slips, which were positioned not in lines, but randomly placed around trees and shrubs to afford privacy and protection from the caustic winds off the Sound.

Zyg and Lu intended the trailer park to be more neighborhood than resort, and searched for permanent, ideally Polish, residents, who shared their work values and devout Catholicism. There were fewer summer people then, the population mostly composed of fishermen and potato farmers. They settled on a veteran, John Saugerties, and his wife as their first, full-time slip renters.

The Kazmierczaks spent their early years in Orient with their only son, Stephan, a reserved but affectionate boy. Heroes they were in their small and simple lives, with Zyg being the best carpenter in town and Lu growing root vegetables and surf-casting for bluefish there on their rugged, lovely beach. They marvelled at the glory of the sea, and often sat on the massive boulders and witnessed how the waves like marching squadrons churned up the green water. They watched the melancholy clouds gracefully wander and rest on Connecticut.

Relished the sometimes surprising warmth of the February sun on their upturned faces.

Their perfect life was threatened when their son hit high school and they were forced to glimpse the man he would become, or rather the type of man. There just wasn't enough sun or distraction or compassion or even vodka to counter their disappointment. Worse yet, his abnormality matured, and they watched in horror as it infected his every gesture and transformed his sweet temperament. The boy had no friends, was often involved in fights, hated athletics. There were no girlfriends. He craved only solitude and his collection of records, colored beach glass, and secondhand postcards from around the world.

Not surprisingly, Stephan ran away to the city before he even completed the eleventh grade. His parents never went looking for him.

Zyg and Lucia wrote the cruel words of their will together; their condemnation would be all the more powerful when spoken from the grave. Their Paradise would be given to the Catholic church in Greenport upon their deaths. The will's executor was their beloved friend and pastor, Father Leon. He was a tall, imposing man with sideburns as dense as chaps on his cheeks, and he shared with them a fondness for vodka, as well as the Lord. They also enjoyed an occasional game of cards. It had been during a hand of Holy Trinity Poker—where king, jack, and ace of hearts beats all—when a soused Zyg conjectured that Paradise Grove might make a fine retreat for the nuns. "It would be like giving paradise back to the Creator," had been his sloshed afflatus.

A messy accident at the intersection of Main and the north road in Greenport would have hastened the transfer of property, had not Lucia managed to survive and to live on long enough to have a change of heart. She amended the will and restored her son as sole heir a year later, not by any great spasm of forgiveness or acceptance, but through a deeper disillusionment with the pastor. On the anniversary of her husband's death, Father Leon had extended his consolation to include the lowering of his pants and the forcing of himself clumsily upon her. Lucia was not flattered by his drunken advance. The thrust of her surf-casting arms sent the priest sailing to his backside, and her admonishments were bathed in a poetic vulgarity that surprised even herself.

And so it was that Stephan Kazmierczak, also known in the East Village of Manhattan as Cherry Pickens, came to inherit Paradise Grove Trailer Court some fifteen years later, when his estranged mother passed from natural causes. Cherry came east to claim her birthright and openly declare to the heavily Republican farming community of the North Fork her sexuality, her style, and her deep resolve.

This was not the boy they had known.

June 5

I undertake the writing of this journal with some hesitation. I know it will accentuate my sinister introversion. And my narcissism.

Cherry says I'm too serious, that I think too much. But solitude does that to you. It has you reliving your thoughts and your dreams in an empty room. You lose a sense of proportion. The line between reality and the imagined becomes a changing thing, like the tide lines. Did it actually happen? Did it happen the way I remember it happening? Did I only dream it?

So for the sake of clarity, I'll record my days, my thoughts, and other trivial things. That's where meaning lies, in the realm of the trivial, where we live the great bulk of our lives.

Like her mother, Cherry is a looker, with the same coloring and strong cheek structure. But she is much taller, with eyes the blue of twilight, and has fuller, more sensuous lips. She has a sexy, smoker's voice although—but for the occasional joint—she no longer smokes.

Beyond Barton, Cherry's other passion is her painted rocks, and she adorns the twelve- to eighteen-inch pieces with elaborate detail. She paints queens at high tea, that is queen with a capital Q, because this is, after all, a trailer park renamed Cherry Grove for the notorious gay resort on Fire Island. These painted ladies are depicted in outrageous assemblages of gowns, jewels, and gloves, with hair heaped high. Cherry utilizes the contours in the stone for jutting hips, breasts, buttocks, and attitude.

She places her creations all around the slips, common areas, and road-sides of the park. It is Barton's responsibility to plant around them, which her lover does systematically in legions of impatiens, pansies, petunias, and sprawling variegated ivies.

Cooking is not a passion of Cherry's, although she does labor at con-vincing Barton that she *can* and actually *does* cook. It is common to see her pedaling her pale-green Schwinn through the day's fading light in search of take-out. It might be from the Blue Light, the Blue Dolphin, or Athenos, but most often, the white bag with the crisp folds at the top is from her friend Paul's fabulous Spiritoso. What a powerful sight it is to see her skimming the earth's flat surface, backlit by a huge setting sun, absorbed in the ancient ritual of the hunt for food.

Once home and removed from plastic and aluminum to china plates, the delicacies of the hunt are served. Paul's food always elicits tender whispers of delight from Barton, and prayers of gratitude for both Cherry and for such brilliant combinations of ingredients as thyme, fava beans, garlic, lamb, and mint.

It touches him that Cherry goes to such lengths to both feed and deceive him, as he knows the same pots and pans live unused in the dish-drainer day after day. These dinners are expensive but, he calcu-lates, they live rent-free, and with her rental income from the park and his investments, they have more money than they could ever spend.

Years earlier, Paul had left the industrial muscle of Detroit in search of a more meaningful, more poetic existence. He'd worked as an engineer at General Motors, and then in a series of odd, unrelated jobs: at a bookstore, a day care center, and then three restaurants. It was in the presence of all that food that Paul found himself. He realized that food was the true metaphor for all things material and spiritual. Food and drink framed all that mattered...be it a chalice of wine, a roasted lamb at Easter, a tomato sun-hot from the vine at noon in August. Meals were shared prayers. He studied at a local culinary school and declared himself a restaurateur in need of a perfect location.

Paul searched for a setting that afforded fresh produce, fish and meats, maybe even local wines, and lots of sun and sea. It must be peaceful but also have an available clientele with cash to spend on the luxury of a unique dining experience.

The North Fork fit the bill. The area was clinging fast to its fishing and agricultural heritages, but was undergoing a transition from potato to grape production in the fields. There were still small, family-owned farms, and scallops and clams in the bay waters. The wealth and excesses of a major metropolitan area were only two hours away.

And so it was that high above an indifferent sea, the forces of the universe provided for Paul an abandoned warehouse on a bluff in Orient, New York for the purpose of establishing his restaurant. The brick structure once had been an oyster-shucking plant and then simply a warehouse for boat engine parts, nothing more elegant than that. It smelled initially of all manner of oils—those from the gelatinous oysters, those from the engine carcasses, and of course, those oozing from the pores of toiling men and women over all those years. Paul had loved that, that this building had past lives, and that they all came with the purchase price.

Paul christened it the *Spiritoso*, so named after the musical direction to proceed in a lively and spirited fashion. The soul-stirring beauty of the location made the price a bargain, with its expansive view of rocky beach, ever-changing combinations of greens and blues in the Long Island Sound, and a fine carpet of sand that introduced again and again, land to sea.

Today, the space has stark interior walls painted a pure, but warm white over the brick. There are no noisy colors in the room, unless they are reflected from the food, wine, or flowers. No bothersome background music. Candles and the sunlight or moonlight from the small, high windows near the roofline are the primary sources of light.

Individual tables line each side of the vast interior, situated far apart, and dressed with white linen. On every table are white candles, goblets, flowers. In the open space in the center of the restaurant, there is a custom-made, thirty-six-foot, narrow table, which provides space for solitary diners. Mimicking the countertop-style camaraderie at roadside diners, this center table allows individuals to eat alone but not be lonely. There is adequate space for both contemplation and conversation.

There are walking and sitting areas outside. Paul had insisted that the view not distract from the color and taste of what was served inside. Consequently, there are no ugly, massive windows, as he has always associated a good view with mediocre food. The sea here is only for anticipating, and later digesting, the meal.

An enormous serving table reigns at the far eastern end of the restaurant. Also covered in white linen, it carries the feast for the day, served between the hours of seven and ten, without reservations. Paul honors his conviction that every diner should be free to choose not only the meat or fish of the meal, but every item accompanying it. Any green, any vegetable, any bread desired can be seen, often even tasted, and combined at the whim of the eater, not the chef.

Because it takes considerable money to eat well away from home, Paul had designed the experience at the Spiritoso to be rich enough to nourish both body and soul. This is embodied in the minimalistic scraps of images on the walls, in the meticulous selection of and respect for the purity of the foods. It is inherent in the incense-like aromas of smoked fish and game, in the fresh vegetables and herb cheeses, and the roasted pignoli of the risotto. There is no set menu and each visit renders a fresh experience. There is an abundance of quiet in the vast space, broken only by the comforting sounds of quiet conversation, the touch of utensils to plates, and corks freed from bottles.

Paul and his wife, Sloan, are now in their third season, with loyal patrons arriving by car, by boat, by foot, and bicycle. The Spiritoso is hard to find—so far off the Main Road and without any advertisement—but impossible to forget.

June 7

June makes a promise. Every year the same one. If I move consciously through this next season, witnessing each detail unfolding, from the lament of the crickets to the majesty of a midafternoon thunderstorm, June will promise this to September and to me: she will replicate a perfect, cloudless, seventy-five-degree June day, the one that makes you feel like a big fat petal on a six-foot sunflower flopping happily in the wind, June will replicate that perfect day in September.

Now I see vivid new growth on many of the pines, bright green shoots of optimism. Even the pyracantha I have espaliered against the shed, denuded at the end of winter of all but its thorns, has returned from the dead and rebudded.

Took the twin lens to Rocky Point early this morning.

The starkness of the winter landscape and a dreary spring have made me hypersensitive to blacks and form. In the last months I've photographed from a strictly structural perspective. Now color has reemerged, the vast blue in the sky, all the pungent greens and creamery yellows, and my vision is saturated to such a degree that I almost lose sight of form. I blurred the focus on my Mamiya. On the small, square viewing screen, I saw Kandinsky during that stage where he seemed caught between representation and abstraction. He painted more passion in his drenching greens and sorrowful blues and blood reds than in his entwined figures in gray, black, and white.

He knew that color is more suggestive when it is freed from form. Color provokes impulse, prods memory, and evokes mood.

Today, I didn't release the shutter but just practiced my seeing. I kept the lens unfocused and moving. As my blurred vision followed the seascape, I absorbed and processed the emotional intensity of each color. My camera searched for the pure essence of each hue . . . the buried resentment in blue, the lust imbedded in violet, calmness in ochre, even the euphoria of immortality in the crisp edge of black. It made no difference if it was sky, or stone, or the foam of the surf.

Take the emotional jumble of a Cézanne blue, so deep and varied with veils of greens, violets, blacks, and powdery wisps of white. I can lose myself in these blues; they seem to contain the entirety of the summer sky and the core of any serenity I have ever known. This one color proves that our perceptions and emotions are never felt independently, but are always a complex melding of things. Remember, it is possible to feel hatred and longing for the same person, and happiness is always, always tinted with sorrow.

Claude lives in a box, a shining silver home on wheels, with no automobile to pull it elsewhere or any desire to go. The Airstream Flying Cloud settles comfortably on the smallest slip of the trailer park.

Today she leaves her trailer and bicycles to Greenport to the Long Island Rail Road station. She plans to ride the train to Riverhead to print at a rental color lab. She hasn't been there in months.

She hopes the ancient diesel train will arrive with a parlor car in tow. This car has a collection of individual seats in loose rows, and extravagances such as cupholders, ashtrays, and red, carpeted walls. Years earlier, from these deep, cushioned seats the elite traveler could lounge and enjoy the sunrise over the potato fields. But over the years the ambiance has degenerated and all that remains is a dingy mix of faux wood paneling and industrial floor carpeting, personalized with cigarette burns and petrified wads of gum.

But today, the 5:30 AM train is not the grand dinosaur she loves, but a new double-decker diesel, compliments of engineers from Japan and General Motors. There is no cigarette smoke–infused parlor car for passengers to enjoy, but rather a new commuting gem as clean as a hospital corridor and with equal personality. The horn is a congested nose blow, not the former proud shriek. Claude thinks that the exterior mimics the clean, simple contours of her Airstream, but the interior in its gray and pastel tones has a sanitary, seamless look that seems to make everyone uncomfortable.

She climbs aboard and soon realizes that she has a superior view of the landscape from the upper seating area on the new train. But as she scans her fellow passengers, she sees that they all are still the same plaid and rugged crowd from Greenport. Claude can't help but feel out of place, a little lost, in her molded seat, as a digital voice announces the stops all the way to Riverhead.

There she walks to Colorworks, a second-floor color darkroom where, for a small hourly fee, she has access to a color enlarger in her own small room and to their communal print processor. After a few hours' work, she pays a small amount more for each of the nine prints she takes home. It's an extravagance for her, but the color accuracy is so critical in her water prints that the cost is justified. She knows that minor adjustments in the filter pack can radically alter the emotional climate of a print. Should it be too emotional, too magenta, she knows (against logic) to add magenta. Too indifferent, too blue? She subtracts yellow. It's second nature.

June 8

Photographs should never be in frames, clamped tight with glass over their faces, and linen tape and mounting tissue restraining their backs. They are not such precious things, but more like thoughts revisited. Photographs should roam freely with you, live with you. They should age with you, with or without grace, even if tomato sauce splatters on them where they are taped up by the stove. Love and abuse them. Stuff them into your pockets so they can be compared to their place of origin. Leave one on a bus, in a pew, or in a public restroom. Set them free and let a stranger ponder their relevance.

NATURE'S LITTLE SLIP-UP

Saugerties steps out from his mobile home and stands guard, feet spread and planted, over his terrain. He had built the small, sturdy deck beneath him. He is the one who has installed and secured the satellite dish in the yard, has shaped every shrub, has even chemically altered the soil to bring a lush lawn to life in the sandy shade.

His fisted hands come to rest on his hips, his white t-shirt taut against the slight bulge of a belly. He is fit for seventy-two, still married, a patriot. Not your typical American male these days; he prides himself on this. He had been in Korea, the war no one really understands or cares about anymore. Had been at No Gun Ri, the greatest misunderstanding of that war. That's what happens when nonmilitary personnel extricate a news story out of a complex situation, he tells himself. Those villagers were decoys, driven into our gunfire by the damn North Koreans. They were the ruthless ones, hiding behind those innocent people, using them as a human shield. *But nobody wants to hear about that.* It had been no easy choice—choice, he knows well, is a luxury a good soldier does not have.

Then again, against his will, he hears the gunfire amplifying, bouncing off the undercarriage of the bridge. And as loud as that is, the screams of the children are louder yet. One little girl...couldn't have been more than five...standing alone, bodies everywhere...

Saugerties stops himself. There had been no choice, only a command.

He hears his wife place the fry pan on the stove. Stands motionless until he hears the hiss of bacon. Talk radio. Smells the heady aroma of coffee.

Better to think how her fingertips had traced those little circles on his low back last night. He had been sleeping but he knew what those circles meant. She still desires him, even if his method is a little abrupt. She had been fast asleep when he returned from washing up. Fifteen years his junior, he is reassured to know she still needs her husband's attention. God hadn't given her children, but he had never held that against her.

Just then, Cherry comes sauntering down the sandy road. His eyes narrow. Except for her long bangs which are draping her eyes, the rest of her hair is tucked neatly beneath a bandanna. She's wearing a short skirt wrapped tightly against her buttocks and thighs. Cherry carries a flat of pink cosmos, and their ferny leaves dance across the patches of sun on the front of her blouse.

She had confused him at first. She was the image of the type of woman he had longed for as a young man, the type of woman you rarely see now—the classic sexiness, the makeup, the done-up hair, the coy acceptance of her supportive role in a man's world. Women now look more like men or don't care how they look at all. They go off to the grocery store in what appears to him to be pajamas.

But here is nature's little slip-up, he thinks, with those full, red lips in sharp contrast to the muscular calves.

He says nothing as she passes. She is repulsive to him for what she pretends to be, that this is somehow normal. It is like the city's gay pride parade come local. *Pride? In what? Decadent abnormality?* He's seen the disgusting ritual on his television. This plague-like influx of homosexuals had managed to raise the bar of tolerance to such a height that any manner of freakish and perverted humanity could claim a right to walk down the middle of Fifth Avenue, with cops protecting them—even gay cops! Reports of bare-breasted women on motorcycles and men in wigs! And now he has to see this perversity here on his own unpaved road.

But Cherry has her own astute perceptions. She can feel the hate-fueled heat of his eyes blaze into her back. And she can easily read his simple mind…standing there on his viewing platform, inspecting the troops, only to find a fairy in their midst. Cherry keeps her eyes focused straight ahead. She has grown resilient. Once your own parents hate you for who you are, the scorn of others is mere child's play. She begins to hum, in her own random way, a little tune from *Carmen*. But once she safely clears his slip, she hears Saugerties launch a wad of spit heavy with disgust in her direction.

Then she turns and meets his eyes. Although she is shaking, she does manage to say in her bravest voice, "Spit all you like, Commander, but you'll never rid yourself of all the hatred in your heart. It'll just fester there until it ends your miserable life."

Saugerties belches a laugh. "My miserable life? You disgusting faggot..." and he lurches forward over the railing of the deck. Before he can continue, Cherry lets her flowers fall from her arms, and turns and runs awkwardly through the hard sand of the road, cursing her three-inch heels and the foolish image she feels she must be conveying.

She thinks about what it would feel like to haul off and slug him, right in his sneering, self-righteous face. *But no,* she says to herself, *no, I run away crying like a girl! Rae would have stood up to him. Couldn't I just pretend to be as big and bad and brassy as Rae. But no, I'm weak. I just walk away when attacked with that kind of bigotry. Because assholes like Saugerties would just as soon beat the life out of a faggot like me as super-size their fries. Without remorse, just like taking out the trash. I hate that bastard. If it wasn't for his poor, sweet wife, I'd have Barton hitch up and haul his ugly aluminum box right out of here. If he thinks he can hurt me, he can't. A person can only be disowned once!*

Finally home, Cherry isn't crying any longer. She sees Barton inside their trailer at the sink. The radio is tuned to that blues station he likes and he is smiling, his head rocking back and forth, hair dancing, eyes half-closed. He is so gorgeous and she knows he loves her. That is all that really matters, isn't it?

June 9

As the poet Louis Zukofsky wrote, "Everything should be as simple as it can be...not simpler." Simplicity must be a complicated matter.

Still, in its pursuit I abandon:
computers
cosmetics
fast food
microwaves
television, cable, satellite dishes
brighteners, dyes, deodorizers
jet skis and SUVs
chewing gum, speed-dialing (that would require a phone)

Formerly on this list were slaughtered animals, but tonight Sonny invited me over for ribs from Spicy's in Riverhead, and I must concede their value. After eating an entire plateful of these rummy, smokey things, I was transported to such a foggy, satiated state that I mistook the meal for a spiritual experience. We ate in a rare silence at their patio table. Even Rae had nothing to say, but toothpicked in deep appreciation bits of the pork from her teeth. I noticed that Six had the same splatters of sauce on her shirt as I did. Her father also made his infamous garlic-infused black beans with yellow rice. I bet the meal's combined aromas sent the whole trailer park into a trance.

Hence I embrace:
food of the simplest nature (except for the above)
nature as the source of inspiration
reuse and compost piles
consuming only what one needs

I don't claim perfection. I am hypocritical in my gluttony for film and paper, darkroom time, chemicals (admittedly, pollutants). Downsizing one's appetite is a process. A little work. A lot of brown rice. Books. No television. Long winters in hibernation.

"You know, Rae, we've been married near a decade now," Sonny tells his wife. She opens a fresh pack of cigarettes and then pours a little more wine into her glass. "God, I'm tired," she sighs as she brings the cigarette to her lips to light.

It is Saturday. The outdoor table is still littered with plates. Thick ridges of the sauces from the black beans and barbecue solidify into dark mosaics on their surfaces. Rae's finger traces one small circle and she licks clean her last taste.

"Where is Six? She could help with this mess," she says.

"Remember back that summer how we'd drive all the way up-island to Medford, to the Hoof & Claw?" her husband asks. "I'd pick you up at your place on 3rd Street."

Rae thinks of Sonny back then, a much leaner man, a roofer he was. He'd show up all scrubbed with Ivory soap and exaggerated politeness. She'd found it refreshing to be in the company of a man who had a little spending money and didn't smell like freshly caught tuna.

"I remember the last time we ate there," is all Sonny has to say for Rae to picture him on that warm September night, a night drenched in a lingering humidity that made her head so foggy and dense, no rational thought could penetrate it.

He had stood on Rae's porch in the drained evening light, his palm against the low tongue-and-groove ceiling, weight on his left hip, a paper-wrapped bouquet of corny carnations encircled by his right arm. She had made him wait, watched him being so pathetically patient there. There with his sincere, sad little flowers—*how she hated carnations!* She had felt no real attraction to him, only a sense of comfort. He had required so little work, and she remembers on that night his long, dark hair against the starkness of his pressed, white shirt. He looked as proper and upright as a Mexican politician.

"I can remember everything we ate and drank that night," Sonny interrupts. "We had stingers to start off. We used to love those. Then we had the calamari with that sweet, spicy sauce, and Chianti, some kind of simple salad, and then lobster tails and steak with baked potatoes, and more Chianti."

Rae closes her eyes, winces. "I felt like I was going to throw up after eating all that shit."

"I know. That's why I ordered you an anisette."

And then while Sonny had rambled on that night about his love for cooking and growing his own food, Rae had been engrossed in picturing their huge meal as it progressed through her digestive track. As a nurse, she knew the strain that so much food and alcohol placed on the system, stimulating the pancreas, the liver, the gall bladder, releasing a floodtide of secretions into the duodenum. She could envision the whole mass of their meal as it chugged through miles of hollow tubing in her gut.

With surprising clarity she now remembers Sonny laying down twenties while she dropped a few rolls into her bag.

"I guess you'll never forget," he continues, "what happened in the parking lot behind that place."

With some mix of horror and repulsion, she does recall the positions they had assumed in their haste once they got to Sonny's '88 F250. Sonny had been cramped on his back on the narrow rear seat of the pickup, with his left boot hanging out the open passenger door. This left the weak ceiling light illuminating her impressive, naked body as it had bounced on top of him, her heavy breasts cupped in his hands.

"I sure wasn't planning on that happening," Sonny says now. "I remember looking up at you. The dome light made your blonde hair a hallo around your face." He smiles and decides not to add the fact that he had never seen, or felt, a woman orgasm like that—with such hunger and bravado. He had almost lost his concentration, so distracted he was by her heaving and shuddering. When he did rally and come, it had seemed as small and unimportant as the dessert they had passed up only a few minutes earlier.

Rae now looks at a rib bone on the ground covered with ants. "Shit no, Sonny, I obviously wasn't planning on that." She had said nothing to him all the way back to Greenport. When he pulled up to her house, she had immediately left his truck, slamming the door behind her, never looking back at him.

"Well, one good thing did come out of it, Rae. C'mon, you have to at least give me that."

The low evening sun is now a crowd of golden figures dancing behind the dark pines. There are sheets still on the line, flapping accusations at her, and there is no more Chardonnay to drown them out.

"Some things are just better off forgotten. I don't know why you're always so dead set on romanticizing a lapse in judgement."

I AM SIX AND I AM NINE

BLESSED BE THE LORD, MY ROCK,
WHO TEACHES MY HANDS BATTLE, MY FINGERS WAR

Psalm 143:1

She is tired of explaining her name. No one ever has to explain a creepy name like Tad or Britney. It had been her own mother who had named her *Six* because of her birth date, the sixth day of the sixth month. Better than *June*, Rae had laughed. Sonny thought it was a name that would force her to defend herself from time to time; this hard name would make her strong.

Six has grown not to care what they call her anyway. Kids pick on her for so many reasons, like her small size, her wild hair, or the fact that she hates to wear a shirt. She feels they are jealous of her, which makes them all the meaner. She can outrun all of them, can catch a bigger fish without trying, and stay underwater for a longer period of time. She knows sacred Sioux chants that can entice rain from a clear sky and calm her mother when she is most irritated. Most kids can't cook an egg let alone separate one. Paul had taught her that.

It baffles her that, even though teachers are supposed to be working on her head, they insist that she wear shoes. Six feels that this is the most unfair of all and proof that they make up rules just because they can. There isn't a pair of shoes made that feel right to her, and they all force her to walk unnaturally. They don't understand that the soles of her feet are like the layered, rugged plates on the underside of a horseshoe crab. She can fly over twigs, razor clams, ice and gravel, carrying her weight more on air than ground. For all these reasons, Mrs. Solak, third grade, and the entire education system hold little interest for the child, with the exception of her one friend, Arthur. He, too, is an outcast and naturally has become her only ally on school property.

Now that Six has the basics of reading and figuring, she is able to read the IGA flyers and sports section, and can compare prices and league standings with Sonny. She is able to quote verses from the Bible better than any Catholic kid, and can carry on a decent conversation with her Creator and all the gods of nature as well. She questions what school has to offer beyond all that.

So Mrs. Solak, I am Six and I am smart enough already, and if you turn your head for longer than three seconds, I am gone.

Paul parks his ancient Mercedes and then sits on the very top step of 67 Steps, the public beach at the end of Sound Road. Far below him, nestled in a collection of large boulders he sees a man with a camera that dangles broken-necked from a tripod mount. After a longer look, he corrects himself. It is a woman.

The camera is aimed at a crevice beneath her, a tiny canyon. Watery sparks fly into the air and the water rushes all around her. She is barefooted and soaked to the belt loops. Paul leans against a railing post as she redirects the camera from time to time, and watches and waits as the earth rotates and the tide gradually changes. At what she must discern to be the right precise moment, she clicks the shutter leaves open to collect the light's reflectance on film. She waits. Again releases. Waits. Many times she does this, only infrequently changing the camera position or advancing the film.

The wind dies but the air cools. The waves stop their roaring and whisper now a slushy lullaby to him. In a daze, he goes back to his car, finds a plaid blanket, wraps it around himself, and returns to continue to watch her there below him. He is content. It is the type of contentment one feels when, as you watch someone engrossed in a task, you sense some participation in that energy, some kinship. She is a soccer game, a porn film, a cooking show. He has no interest in what she's doing. He is simply interested in watching her.

Paul begins to anticipate her body movements. He plays a little game, trying to guess what she will do next. When will she drag her fingers through her short, damp hair again? When will she roll those trouser legs a little higher? When will she pick up the notebook, look for her pen, sit on the boulder to write? Will she ever raise her eyes to look at him watching her? He vows not to look away if she does.

She does not. He must get to the farmer's market. He stands, turns, leaves. She watches him go.

June 11

create images on film that cannot otherwise be seen

the image is etched into the film emulsion, drawn by light and the passage of time

time is the abstracting element

f22 at 1/250

f22 at 1/125

f16 at 1/125

eight exposures, careful sequencing, build image upon image, freeze water's movement, make it fluid, keep it fluid, make it alive

hints of the fiction of time's passing, like memory itself, which is a compilation of events divorced from the present, from reality

nature's emotions range from rage to melancholy, don't know what will rise to the film's surface or where it comes from

can't say whether the emotional impact delivered through the resulting image is bared by the lucid waters, the light of the sun, or extracted from me somehow

I hate being watched

the elements
eternal and ever-present water, coastal pebbles, rocks, boulders, sand, bits of mock-ancient oyster shells and clam jackets, wisps of black seaweed

allow the water to soften and make fluid all that is hard and imperme-able...what would normally take decades with the sea's persistent wearing away of mineral-rich rock and debris will, through the illusion of time and movement recorded on film, occur within a minute or two

black and white is different in that line, tone, and composition carry the entire weight of the image's success...exposure time must be accurate or you are left with a muddy, flat mess, without good contrast and clean whites with detail

I choose some elements, others choose me, but where I place my tripod and what then flows into the viewfinder...that's much like life...there's what you intend and then there's what happens.

A SACRED PLACE

Catalino "Sonny" Gutierrez is Mexican-American, spiced with Lakota ancestry. Golden skinned with blue-black hair, he is broad across the shoulders and the rest of his torso follows at an equal girth. He has shared little of his earlier life with Rae, but his daughter knows how he carries his past in each step he takes: his childhood in Nebraska, his Mexican father, his Sioux mother, the wisdom of Wakan Tanka.

For some reason unknown to him, he never sleeps well. Even after a half-dozen beers, when sleep comes on him fast and deep, it never lasts more than a few hours. Then he's up again, checking on Six or out in his garden, picking beetles off the bush beans by flashlight.

It doesn't help that Rae works five nights of the week, sometimes even extra hours so that she doesn't even see Six before school. On the weekends, Sonny does sleep better, comforted by his wife's soft flesh tight against him. He nestles into the silky, pink curves of her like a babe in the womb, lost in the chimeric dreams of the unborn. The bed feels comfortably cramped with Rae in it; their bodies are always touching in some way. But even then, he's only good for three or four hours and then he's awake again, anticipating each of her shuddering breaths as she sleeps. He ponders odd, irrelevant things while he lies there next to her. *What is it like to live as a fetus inside another's body? Does a fetus dream? When she was in Rae's womb, did Six dream, hear his voice, feel the warmth of his hands when he caressed Rae's belly? Or, because she was unblemished by experience, did she tap into universal knowledge? Did she experience Wakan Tanka?*

Sonny spends many hours of the night worrying about his daughter. He knows she is a child of the wandering wind and must find her own way, and that is fine with him. She is like the wind and the clouds. Now he realizes that he should have given her an Indian name, something beautiful like Wind Driven Cloud. The name Six was a joke, Rae's joke. Maybe he'll start calling her Cloud. It bespeaks her airy nature; she is so contemplative and spiritual, not like other children. For this he is grateful.

On this June morning, he is up before the sun. He wears only terry cloth shorts, their drawstring tied beneath his wide, rounded belly. He walks outdoors barefooted and inspects his land. He cares little for the mobile home with its false grandeur—the plastic moldings, the flat roof, the vinyl siding. There is nothing of nature in it, no real wood, even the bed coverings are synthetic. But when the soles of his feet touch dried leaf, fragrant pine sap, and earth, and he feels the soft, feminine touch of the predawn wind, he is truly home.

Sonny appreciates the odd design of this trailer park. Most he's seen have the mobile homes all lined up straight on tiny slips of land. The lots at Cherry Grove are large and irregular, plenty wooded for privacy while still maintaining a neighborhood feel. He knows his neighbors, the year-rounders, even the summer people. Cherry isn't as rule-minded as her mother was, just wants folks to peacefully coexist. Now, pretty much anything goes on your own slip, but she insists you keep it clean, no visible trash or abandoned cars on cinder blocks.

On his roughly 90-by-120-foot parcel Sonny knows each of the twenty-three trees that grow there, every leaf tree and evergreen. He loves the laurels, junipers, pink-flowering azalea and hollies, those that thrive and those that struggle. He pampers the weak with compost and manure and soapy baths to free them of infestations. He is always planting, taking great pleasure in the process. He prunes sparingly, prefers a natural shape to things, and burlaps the delicate specimens against the harsh winter winds off the Sound.

Now he wanders over to the only consistently sunny spot on his property, beyond the chicken coop on the elevated south corner, to a small garden he has enclosed with a fence made of cedar posts and juniper limbs. He admires the garden gate he has made with bleached beach wood, ornately entwined with grape vines. It has a pyramidal top pointing towards the sun, and an attached twig planter. There he plants the annual sweet pea vines that will dot the gate with color come midsummer.

Inside the fence is his raised-bed, vegetable garden. There are two low, wooden stools with an oval cut-out on each top, so father and daughter can tote them about as they work. This is, they agree, a magical and sacred place. Sonny has transformed the soil from a sandy, empty substance into an richly organic loam, blessed with compost and buried fish heads. No harsh pesticides nor synthetic fertilizers ever touch this place and everything thrives, except cucumbers. They are doomed to develop the mildew that devastates most Long Island, organically grown cukes. He is working on finding the one type that is resistant enough to produce what they need.

This year, Sonny is growing 'Red Sun' and 'Orange Blossom' tomatoes. There are 'Vermont Cranberry' bush beans, a purply Swiss chard, and common iceberg lettuce because it tastes the best on tostadas. He always grows cilantro, basil, sage, and the garlic that Rae seems to like on everything but chocolate cake. There will be a little corn this season and Six's favorites, flashy scarlet runner beans and crooked neck squash. By mid-August, it will all be a tangled, overgrown, beautiful, bountiful mess.

As the first terra cotta tones hit the sky on this perfect morning, Sonny sits on his stool in the garden's center, face to the rising sun, toes buried in the warming soil. He straightens his back and pulls up his chin. He has so much, he thinks, has all of this, and Rae, and his beautiful, wild Wind Driven Cloud.

He watches as the sun climbs in the sky over his small but vital world. Sonny then falls into a sleep as deep as it is uncomfortable, his back rounded and his chin resting on his noble chest. He is such until Six stretches her body against his back, begging for breakfast.

Rae is out annoying the plump hens, fingering beneath them for Six's breakfast. Sonny already has the bacon on.

"I prefer my eggs in nice, clean cartons, right out of the IGA," she tells the chickens, "so don't be thinking this is any fun for me either." They squawk and bitch until Rae stands back from them, palms to hips, and hollers back, "Hey listen, I'm no different than you. Just another large, loud female from Long Island!"

"With the hair to prove it," Cherry adds as she walks past. "And you still owe me for last month, case you forgot, Miss Clara Barton."

"Yow, speaking of Barton, how is that fine boy you call yours?"

"Outta your league," Cherry calls back to her.

"Oh, but I have a large, all-encompassing league," Rae counters.

"That would be the entire North Fork with the occasional foray into the balance of Suffolk County," Cherry says and they both laugh. Rae never takes offense when allusions are made to her sexual prowess. With the face and features of a model a little past her prime and off her diet, she is stunning just the same.

"Ouch!" Rae jokes and snatches an egg. "I'll send Six over with the money."

Once in the kitchen, she cracks the egg into the frying pan and ponders her daughter's legendary truancy. Last week her teacher had called to explain that should Six miss even a minute more of school in these final days, she would have the pleasure of repeating the whole grade. Six had promised to abide by that ruling. "I'll go but I hate school," Rae remembers her saying. "I can teach myself everything I need to know."

Rae had intended to respond with a profound statement about the value of education and good grades and learning to get along with other children. Unfortunately, all that actually passed her lips had been "*Wrong!* My taxes pay these people to teach you what they think you need to know. And if you don't get your clever little butt there on a regular basis, *I will* find a source of employment for you. There are plenty of immigrant nine-year-olds digging potatoes and picking peaches and washing dishes. You can bet your ass they'd rather be in school. You can ask your father if you don't believe me."

She hadn't intended to throw down a threat like that, but the primal tendency toward fear induction won out.

But now, breakfast is ready and Rae refuses to have that fight again. "Six, get out here. Eat your breakfast and then we have some work to do before your father drives you to school."

The girl appears bare-chested, wearing short, suede britches, decorated with beads.

"Where on God's green planet did you find those pants? You look like a wild Indian child. But not to worry because Mama's getting you ready for school today and when you march out of here, you will be clean, combed, and in this dress."

Out of a plastic Swezey's bag comes what looks like a child prostitute's dress, a garish purple affair that glimmers like metal in the unnatural light cast from the range hood. The color is offset by an oversized white collar and pink, fake-fur buttons. Adding to Six's horror are a pair of pink vinyl sandals, placed like two dead bodies on the shag carpet.

"Now this outfit makes a statement, Six. It says 'I am a confident and pretty girl. I am unique, feminine, and strong.' Why, Mrs. Solak will think overnight you've become…"

"Your mother!" Sonny walks into the kitchen, also wild-haired and bare-chested. "Don't you worry, Six, you're not wearing that thing."

The child is still staring at the dress.

"It's okay, Sonny. I'll wear it," Six finally says.

"Good." Rae doesn't believe her; this can't be that easy. So she reinforces her case, "Because if you are not unique, and pretty, or interesting at all, you will end up with an uncivilized man no better than your father."

"You know, Rae, that might of hurt the first time you said it, but you've gone and used it so many times, your blade's dull. Anyway, it matters more what the child thinks of herself, not what some damn boy thinks of her." He gets right into Rae's face to finish, in his softest, sweetest voice, "And as pretty as you may be, my sexy little hen, you still gotta work nearly everyday and crawl into bed with me when you're done."

Six senses a fight coming on. "Mama, I'll go get washed up. I ain't that hungry anyway. Sonny'll drive me to school, okay?" At least, she thinks, she has a plan.

"Nice try, baby. Mama will drive you this morning. Now get into the shower."

"I ain't wearing that dress!" Six screams. "I'd rather walk in there plain naked than wear that. They'll all laugh at me. Remember when they put that crown of thorns on Jesus' head and made fun of him? That's what those kids'll do to me. That ugly, ugly dress is gonna be my crown of thorns."

"Well, since you brought up religion, Six, do you remember the fourth commandment, 'Honor thy mother and thy father'!" She's screaming now. "You will do what I tell you to do, which is to go to school in that dress and I will personally watch you walk into Oysterponds Elementary. End of story."

Six looks at Sonny. She says softly, knowing she's already lost, "Can't I just honor my father?"

"Get!" Rae roars at the child.

"This is cruel, Rae," Sonny says. "Those kids are gonna eat her alive and you know it."

"As you always tell me, my love, she'll be the stronger for it."

HOME SCHOOLING

"DO NOT JUDGE, AND YOU SHALL NOT BE JUDGED;
DO NOT CONDEMN, AND YOU SHALL NOT BE CONDEMNED;
FORGIVE, AND YOU SHALL BE FORGIVEN"

Luke 6:37

"Today is not a school day?" Paul is washing greens and doesn't turn to look at his small friend.

Six takes a seat. "They called me a gypsy and a faggot. They said it's 'cause I live in a trailer and I got dark skin and I have this faggot dress. They all laughed at me and I hate them, so I took off. Nobody even saw me. I don't even know what those names mean."

Then Paul does turn to look at her as he wipes his hands on his apron. He does not laugh though he wants to. He manages a sad, sympathetic smile. The girl still wears the horrid dress and there are lumpy waves in her hair. He assumes it must have been braided. There are faint, uncharacteristic scents of talcum powder and soap, but she also is as she always is…dirty, barefoot, defiant.

"Well, let me get a good look at you. I would describe your beautiful skin color as that of rich sand, just touched by the sea. They're jealous of that I'm sure. And you have a lovely home with your father's wonderful garden."

Then Paul drops to one knee and touches the hem of her dress. "But this dress should be burned immediately. Your usual clothes are more appropriate for a child in constant motion. As for being a gypsy, well, I'd be complimented if I was called that. A gypsy is a magical person. She owns only the belongings she can carry with her. And, a gypsy loves music and trickery. So I think this name fits you well."

Paul stands and walks in a circle around her. "But, do I see before me a faggot? I think that name was inspired by your fanciful dress. You know, I also have been called cruel names. I think we should do a little research, just to get to the bottom of this."

Paul takes her hand and leads her to the bookcase near the fireplace. He pulls from the lowest shelf a black dictionary with gold printing on the cover.

"Is it your Bible?" Six asks.

"Sort of. I mean if you love words as I do."

He sits her in a rocker and then flips through the pages of the book.

"Ah, here it is. *Fagot*. A bundle of twigs tied together and used as fuel. You're certainly not a bunch of twigs. Oh, but *faggot* with two *g*'s is another thing altogether. That was a nasty name for a woman in the sixteenth century, so you're off the hook there. Or it can also mean a male homosexual, so that definitely leaves you out."

The child still has a confused look.

"Six, do you know what a homosexual is?"

She shakes her head.

"It's simply a man who loves another man. Like Cherry."

"Cherry is a girl."

"Hmm, more true than not. Enough of this lesson. But, you can see, can't you, how important it is to know what words mean before you use them?"

"Yeah, because then you can show kids how stupid they are. Maybe I'll ask Sonny for one of those word Bibles."

"Good. Now go into the bathroom and take off that frock of yours and I'll go get you a big t-shirt to wear."

When they are both back in his kitchen, Paul continues his instruction. "Let's get to the matter of you not being in school today, which seems to happen a lot with you, I hear. That's much more serious than silly name-calling. I won't turn you in, but I insist on conducting another lesson right here in this kitchen."

The layout of Paul's cottage varies from most. Often, homes on the water position their living room to face the sea, so one can watch the gulls flutter about or track the sun's glorious appearance and disappearance from the comfort of their sofas. But at Paul's, it's the kitchen that commands the prime water view. There's a wall of simple double-hung, wooden windows of the rattling, sticking variety, and just beyond, over the grasses, lies the moody Long Island Sound. This day, a vast audience of sea and gulls and clouds witness the labors of the barefoot teacher and his likewise barefoot pupil.

Paul brings Six to the kitchen table and strokes his goatee while surveying his cookbooks. "We will read and measure and write down our modifications. That should cover your three r's."

Six swings her feet beneath the table and smiles as she stares at the Sound. Paul hands her a small bowl of grapes.

"Of His fullness we have all received," she says and she tosses one into her mouth.

"Amen and alleluia," Paul answers. "Now read me the ingredients for the salad."

During the next half-hour, Six sings out the quantities of romaine, parsley, tomato, toasted pine nuts, and chives. She scavenges ingredients from the cupboard and refrigerator and adds words to the modified recipe. There are purply black olives and white balsamic vinegar, an olive oil robust with the woody taste of the olive's pit, fresh pepper and sea salt, bits of a garlicky hard salami, and a slightly pungent yet child-friendly cheese. They chop it all into small pieces so that, as Paul tells the girl with great seriousness, "every bite is complete." When he finishes lecturing on the importance of harmony and balance in cooking, she asks, "Like in gospel singing?" And Paul agrees, "Yes, very much like that."

Once they've cleaned up the kitchen, the two sit across from each other at the table with the large bowl of salad between them. Paul pours a Chardonnay for himself and freshly made lemonade for his guest. They eat from the bowl together. They devour every bit—she eating way more than he does—except for the bowl of salad they save in the refrigerator for his wife. She is already at the restaurant but will not eat there. This reminds Paul to explain to Six the importance of feeding the ones you love, that it's a form of love, a sacred act, like what her father does for her.

"Like Jesus did with the bread and fishes," Six adds.

Once they finish eating, since at this hour school will be half over anyway, they retire to the patch of warm sand they favor, amidst the sea grasses beyond the kitchen windows. They fall asleep there in the sun, both brown, both satisfied and floating on the soft, white towels beneath them toward a fantasy land of fanciful gypsies and good health.

RED

When he awakens she is gone. He feels like he's lost his wallet or his keys; he is that disoriented without her. All that remains of the child is the crumpled t-shirt he'd given her to wear. Paul wonders if she is running naked through the pines like the wild child she so wonderfully is. He smiles and slowly rises to his feet. The day has grown warmer. He should go soon to the restaurant.

Inside the cottage he finds Sloan sleeping on the daybed in their screened-in sitting room. She wears only red cotton shorts. She lays on her side facing him, her hair covering her eyes. Her breasts look fuller in this position, her hips sharper, and her thighs are like bulging loaves of unbaked bread. He knows how sexy she must look but cannot feel it; he is too crippled by her vulnerability.

He finds paper, a pen. He sits on the floor only a few feet from her. He writes:

Red

In red's perfect lushness
I became an eager boy
loved my Rockettes
my Corvettes
loved sex and speed and carelessness.

But what is red to an older man?
A steak, a skirt, the flag, the Wings?
Banners and burning and bloodstained things?

That would not be this older man.

I believe in red as romance and ripe affirmation,
a strawberry on June's midriff, bedded in straw,
the way it feels in my mouth, before tasting.

No, better
that red berry between your red lips.
No, better yet
half that berry between your lips,
the other between mine.

He stops. Feels himself losing her. He adds at the bottom of the page:

You are as life-affirming to me as the early days of summer,
when summer seems inextinguishable.
You are the first strawberry I ever ate, and the last.
You are fields of strawberries for endless seasons.
You linger in my mind as the taste lingers in memory,
more luscious, more red, than in reality.

He then folds the paper twice and takes it to the box in his drawer. Before he puts it away, he opens it up again and adds one more thing at the top of the page:

You hate poetry. You would rather be reading a summons.
I like to think these are for you. Maybe they are only for me.

When he returns to his wife he kisses her gently on the lips to wake her. Her lips are not sweet, but dry and salty. He feels intensely his love for her. It makes him weak and lightheaded. They must leave soon, he tells her.

June 13

I slept on the beach last night.

Was at the Whiskey Wind. There way too late, drinking Sam Adams, boring strangers to tears with my rantings about color and emotion and being fluid. I'm sure I was brilliant or made no sense at all. I remember this weak-chinned man, the top of his head bald but he had long hair ringing the periphery, as if to compensate. More details emerge from the fog…his finger-tips sometimes stroking my neck as he massaged my back, how I studied the grain of the oak curve of the bar beneath my cheek as he worked my muscles into a fluid state. Ah, there's my fluidity again. I must have raised my head because I remember seeing the green light illuminating the bottles behind the bar and my face in the mirror there, looking the color of a municipal swim-ming pool. Then I noticed numbers inked on the back of my hand, no name, just four numbers, a local guy. Such a sad, wonderful night of wiping clear the space between my ears and filling it instead with wood veneer and lip-stick smears on glasses and the wisdom in a posted sign, "Some call it a six pack, I call it a support group." This stranger touching me and a fiddler named McCamy playing brilliantly and beer arriving unbeckoned and it was the Greenport I love, offering all a tattered sense of belonging, real or imagined…who cares? Feels the same.

Still I was over the edge. Too much, and then a couple shots of tequila beyond too much. Angry with myself for that. I rode my bike, ever so cau-tiously and none too straight, not home but to the park. Could I have been arrested for a BWI? Lay on my back in the cold sand to clear my head. There, lulled by the surf, blanketed by starlight, dizzy and nauseous, I slept the little night left.

It was barely dawn when I came to and sensed the remorse and beer fer-menting in my bowels. Low back numb. Eyes stinging from the sparks of sunlight on the horizon.

That's when I saw them. I thought it was two women, maybe two men, maybe one of each. They were of equal height and similar build, wearing loose clothing, and shimmering and sauntering like holy men. With the sun-rise backlighting them, I thought I was about to be visited by twin saints.

I didn't move and remained with my cheek in the sand, mesmerized by the approaching figures from the east. Jesuses come to heal the debauched and dying sinner.

A gentle wind rustled their garments about them. I thought of gulls slowly flying from pilings. I somehow knew it was a man and a woman, but I wasn't quite sure which was which. That seemed strange, but it was their interaction that marked them as a pair.

All this made me feel that I might still be drunk.

As they neared me, I became aware of my appearance. I must have looked like litter from the Whiskey Wind blown all the way to this beach. My only white shirt was opened to the waist and as wrinkled as a bed sheet. My khakis were stained with someone else's wine. I wiped the dribble from the corner of my mouth, ran my fingers through my hair, and sat up.

They came closer. They were such beautiful people. That is, beautiful in their juxtaposition to each other... his deep caramel-colored skin and her being fair and blonde. He was soft, airy whereas she was dense and rooted to the ground. A poet and an iron worker.

They said nothing to me as they passed, but the dark poet did look back in my direction and he smiled. It wasn't a mean smile, I don't know, somehow I did not feel judged, more like forgiven for my excess. My eyes stayed on them as they continued on past me, now with the low sun painting their backs in gold. And after a minute or so, she did turn, the iron worker, and she stared at me but did not smile.

WHO SHE IS

"Who is she?" They are back at their cottage, preparing breakfast.

Paul answers with a question. "The remnants on the beach?"

"Yes. What happened to her? Did you smell her?"

Paul cuts a cantaloupe in half. He scoops the seeds into the compost bucket on the counter. He prefers not to revisit the smell on the woman.

"I saw her photographing at 67 Steps a couple days ago," he says. "I'd say today she was hugely hungover."

Sloan reaches for the bowls. "She looks familiar."

"My sweet, this is the North Fork. Throw a stone in any direction and you'll beam someone you know, or at least someone who knows someone you know. That's the beauty, and the downside, of living here."

"I think she sits in that little house at the beach."

"Then you already know who she is," Paul says. He ladles yogurt into the melon halves, sprinkles that with blueberries.

Sloan is now behind him and with her hands on his hips pulls him into her. She wraps her arms around him. He feels the warmth of her breath on his neck, the soft flesh of her breasts against his back. His fingertips come to rest on the cool tile of the countertop. He steadies himself. This is when they would have made love.

"Maybe we should befriend the poor thing," he says.

Sloan says nothing, but as she pulls away from him, he swears he hears a slow tearing sound. He hopes it had been only the noise made by her dry feet skimming the linoleum.

Rae goes on and on about the accident and the flames, "hell come to earth" and such. She describes the flames as being so intense you can see them clearly with your eyes shut. She explains that a tractor-trailer traveling east carrying 8,500 gallons of gasoline had been struck head-on by an old Chevy van.

Six eats up every word, sitting there at her feet, legs crossed. Her mouth hangs open.

"I heard nothing about this on NPR, but that's not us, that station is on the South Fork," Cherry says, sitting across from Rae. She too looks a little ragged this morning; she hasn't yet addressed the morning shave or makeup. She still manages to exude a raw femininity, drawn by her full lips, her delicate cheekbones, and demeanor. "I'll explain the difference," she adds. "The North Fork is outlets. The South Fork is Rodeo Drive. News here is an accident such as this. News there is when a celeb in an SUV rams into a crowd outside a nightclub."

"Don't be too harsh, love. We all have our excesses." Rae wants to go on with her story and is smoking more than usual.

"After impact the rig came to rest about 100 feet away, right at Gina Tarrow's Gulf station," Rae says, and then reaches for a cigarette. "The driver got out just before the cab went up in a blaze. Of course, the driver of the van was killed on impact. I guess he fell asleep, or was just plain drunk. He crossed into the opposite lane and hit the rig near dead on."

The hospital had rushed Rae and some other staff over with the EMS crew just in case things got out of hand, what with the cab blazing away and the tanker, Gina's pumps and buried tanks all right there. Six stares at the long tale of smoke that pours from her mother's lips. "Could have been an explosion big enough to make an island out of Orient," Rae says calmly.

As she goes on with her elaborate and likely somewhat exaggerated tale, Cherry is distracted by the whole show that is Rae. After all she'd been through last night, Rae had taken on an attractive ruggedness. Her uniform is the usual pressed, white t-shirt and men's white trousers, with an ornate, bejeweled belt arching over her solid hips. Cherry thinks the tale sounds a little made up, but there is a substantiating, thin layer of soot on her skin and clothing, as well as a single dot of blood on her left cuff. One shoe is unlaced and her eye shadow is smeared, as if she had dragged her arm across her face to wipe away perspiration or fatigue. She has, Cherry observes, the look of a certain actress she can't quite name who always looked especially sexy when dirty and torn up. *Was it Jane Russell? Barbara Stanwyck? That sassy Geena Davis?*

She sees that Rae's hair is characteristically piled on her head, but it's all knotted up and sticky, in a very irregular shape. The hair on the backside of her head is especially tangled, like she had been on her back at some point during the night. This, she knows, is highly likely and then validated by what Rae says next.

As Cherry tunes back into Rae's monologue, she is going on about the cool composure of Bullet Hayes, a handsome EMT who had worked with her on the rig's driver. The driver miraculously had only minor head injuries, as far as they could tell on the scene. Rae emphasizes again their great fear that the tanker's flammable cargo might explode. They had dangled at the brink of catastrophe, she says, but stayed on until their work was done. A one-mile area had needed to be evacuated. The neighborhood, and especially the rescue workers, had been in constant danger.

When she winds up her tale, Six wraps her arms around her mother's neck and curls her legs around her hips. Laughing now, Rae stands and climbs the steps to their home with the child still affixed.

"Off to school with you, my little monkey," Rae says. "Don't want poor Mrs. Solak getting her hopes up thinking she won't have to deal with you today."

June 14

They appeared again, the two witnesses to my fall from grace yesterday morning. Now that I've recovered from my hangover, I realize that I have seen them around. He is my stalker from 67 Steps. They're friends with Cherry. I remember seeing them walk the beach together. He has a restaurant, very pricey, on the Sound. An odd place, some sort of Soho warehouse knock-off. Now I remember Cherry called him the Dalai Lamb-a. She loves his lamb. And she labeled his companion a bit of a stick, that interesting.

Six knows them too, but I can't recall how.

But today, the dark chef appeared at my booth and simply said, "Walk with us awhile." It wasn't an invitation, more like a dare. He turned before my answer and began walking east in a slow, measured way. His companion, the stick, stood motionless, staring at me rudely, so I hurried to catch up with him, just to relieve the pressure of her eyes. She hurried past me and we formed a line of quiet soldiers patrolling the deserted beach. She has peculiar hair, very yellow, cropped in chunks as though she had grabbed handfuls and cut it herself.

We walked around the next curve and then sat, the three of us, in individual cups of a massive boulder right at the sea's edge. He did turn and smile once in my direction, but other than that I could have been there alone, watching the waves splash around me. Wished I had my camera. I needed something to do.

Then we walked back and they left me at my booth with a wave goodbye from him and nothing from her.

It was all so odd, but I do appreciate the respite from the small talk that might normally fill strangers' time together. He has an intense but comfortable presence. I imagine I might come to know him without words, maybe sense his past in his silence.

WHY THE EGGS WENT COLD

COME TO ME, ALL OF YOU WHO LABOR AND ARE BURDENED,
AND I WILL GIVE YOU REST.

Matthew 11:28

Another morning, bright as a new toy, too perfect to be locked indoors. The child bares her teeth in a triumphant snigger as she works her way from the back of the school to the Sound. Her arms swing in perfect rhythm as her feet fly low just above the ground. This pleases Six. She relishes the stretch in her arch and the light placing of the ball of each foot as it grazes the surface, slicking over pavement and grass and then sand, weaving around broken glass, dog shit, upturned clam shells. She is the running. She is the rare east wind. She is as liquid a movement as are powerful sea currents passing between shore and sandbar.

Six keeps her eyes focused straight ahead, and doesn't need to watch what dangers may lie in her path—her feet have their own wisdom and she lets them find safe passage. She thinks of her father's stories about walking on hot embers, how you separate body from thoughts.

Flying now over the beach, her shirt comes off easily, like old skin from a snake. She does think to tuck it into the waist of her shorts, in the back. There will be enough hell to pay without the loss of clothing.

Soon she sees the Blue Light ahead. It will be a gamble, she knows. Mrs. Rose sometimes harbors and feeds her, but she is unpredictable. There might be kitchen work or worse, a trip back to Oysterponds. But she is hungry now, and must get on the good side of the lady.

• || •

Rose's Blue Light Diner sits Soundside just west of the causeway in East Marion, tucked back away from the Main Road just a bit. Her six blue lanterns out front serve as beacons to locals and lost souls alike, but all receive the same abrupt treatment from Rose, proprietor. You may not always get what you order, as a directive such as this is quite common: "Benjamin Cupps, you had eggs and sausage yesterday. You get oatmeal and a banana today. Sit!"

That "sit" is also barked at anyone who might be standing around, perusing the handwritten menu or peering in the front windows. Her index finger is thrust downward as her eyes meet the diner's. Rose condones no rude or indecisive behavior from her patrons.

Her dyed black hair is her only deception. She has a large, padded frame straightforwardly represented in boldly printed, colorful dresses. No makeup. No excuses. "You get what you get" is printed clearly right on the menu.

There are few complaints, however, as the cuisine at the Blue Light is undeniably delectable and as diverse as the diners. Witness the sea bass ceviche, all lime and cilantro, served with chunks of sweet potato, a hunk of corn on the cob, and papery slices of red onion. This Blue Light classic had been concocted by Rose's Peruvian spouse, a person rarely seen at the diner. On the menu, too, are fish chowders; mixed-berry pies; a fiery, black-bean chili; and pineapple ice cream sodas. The breads are baked daily and the coffee is so strong the menu contains a medical caution for those with heart irregularities.

As the cost for and availability of her ingredients fluctuates, Rose offers no fixed meal prices. She figures in her head what she feels is fair and people are accustomed to that. No one has ever been scolded for not having enough to pay. It is rumored that non-locals are quoted slightly higher prices. Rose often can be seen appraising the vehicle the customer drives up in to fine-tune her calculations. This makes a late-model Lexus owner's meal pricier than the same for the driver of a 1984 VW camper.

On this Monday morning as Six nears the diner, Rose has already had it with the pushy Manhattan crowd. One couple had overstretched their weekend and pranced in with their cell phones attached to their heads, barking their take-out orders like her place was a Burger King. Then the man had unwisely complained, "I can get a cheaper cup of coffee in the city."

"Well, then go get it there and kiss my hash browns on your way out!" Rose had screamed right in his face.

Then she had cleared the whole restaurant with "Get out! Get out! Oh my God, the kitchen's on fire!" The local folks know by now that this means to go sit in their vehicles for a couple of minutes, and to come back in once the BMWs and all the *citiots* (as Rose calls them) have pulled away.

Rose then slams the door after all that ruckus and is taken by surprise by the bare-chested child.

"Shit, honey, you scared me," she yelps.

"I'm sorry, Mrs. Rose. Didn't mean to."

"Soooooo…you busted loose again, did you? You know if I don't hustle your little butt back to Oysterponds, your mom'll have at me. That's never fun."

"Please don't do that," Six pleads. "I'm so hungry. Can I get some toast and honey? I could help with breakfast clean-up for you, you know."

"Little Miss Six, I got a cop in there right now eating his eggs cold so he isn't in that great a mood. He'd probably enjoy driving you back to school himself."

Six takes a second. "I could eat in the kitchen."

"All right, come on in." The child has a way of making her irrational, always able to bring out the rebel in her. "But then you sneak yourself back over to school, agreed?" Rose says.

"Yes, ma'am. I promise."

"You promise? Well, I'm skeptical, baby. Where are your shoes? And you'll need to wear your shirt properly, too. This is a respectable joint and both shirt and shoes are required, even in the kitchen."

June 19

Had a disturbing morning after a full night of rain.

Was alone in my booth, listening to the mesmerizing alto chanting of the rain on my roof and on the Russian olive and bayberry leaves outside. Such a delicate and lovely sound.

For some, rain induces melancholy. For me, it just brings on a lazy intro-spection, all dreamy and disjointed, like I'm never fully awake.

A battered, white Cadillac was in the parking field not far from my booth, less than 100 feet away. Paper bags and some clothing were stuffed up by the rear window and on the dashboard. The driver's side window was opened a crack and a cardboard beer carton heavy with rain sat just outside. A few empty cans were rolling like little boats in a puddle nearby. Probably parked there most of the night.

The window in the back seat was also rolled down a bit and I could see movement inside the car. A figure, a woman. She was on her knees in the rear seat, the top of her head faced me, her long, loose hair hanging. She started to rock on her pelvis. Her palms came up to brace on the roof of the car. Once she was upright I saw her breasts, stark, white apparitions swaying behind the fogged window as she rotated and plunged.

I kept watching. Her movements changed from the stirring motions to a faster, piston-like bubbing. Her hands lowered to hook on the top edge of the open window, which clunked down a few inches more with her weight. This startled her and broke the reveling trance she was in and her eyes rose. She was gripping the glass, taking the thrusts from beneath her without counter-ing. Then her eyes locked with mine. She watched me watching her.

I don't look away. Some sickening mixture of shame and excitement immo-bilized me. I remembered to breathe, but kept on staring as a long minute more passed and the rain stopped or it didn't.

Only the slightest narrowing of her eyes and a small lowering of her chin marked her orgasm. And then the little smile, accusing and so coy, she gave to me. Or to him? His hands came up into her tangled hair and he pulled her body back down to him.

I pulled on my old raincoat, over my head. The zipper's been jammed for years. I walked to the bluff on the eastern edge of the park. Made note of increasing erosion. Walked back.

The rain stopped abruptly, the Cadillac was gone, a drier patch marked its former position on the surface of the lot. Reminded me of a chalk line around a victim's body.

CHANEL AND PHEROMONES

Rae has left the hospital and is driving east when the wind finally seduces the rain from the heavy cloud cover. Funny how the weight of the sky seems to lighten the burden of a long night, she thinks. How she does love to sleep while it rains. Each hollow beat on the roof of the trailer will soon be a gentle massaging of her forehead, her spine, the soles of her feet. The mayhem and the boredom of the ER will be tapped away moment by moment as she drifts to sleep. She can almost feel Sonny's comforting, yeasty breath warm on her breast. Six, heaven willing, at school. *Perfection.*

It is 4:00 in the afternoon when she wakes. The rain has stopped, but what a mess it has left behind. Rae stands at the trailer door, her robe wrapped tightly around her. Pools collect around the legs of their patio table and she watches cigarette butts float aimlessly in a rain-filled ashtray. She finds the whole scene depressing, and drags herself under the mobile home's awning and lands in a plastic chair that is just shy of dry. It is unpleasant, the dampness slowly soaking her bottom, but she's too tired to address it. She lights a cigarette and pulls on it, curling the smoke deep into her lungs. She hadn't slept well; odd dreams had plagued her. It is only Wednesday.

She is starving. *Where is Sonny?*

The cigarette helps to rouse her a bit. Rae notices that Cherry has just completed another work of rock painting. *The crazy drag queen, does she actually think of it as art?* The gaudy thing sits at the end of Rae's driveway, and now she sees a figure, huddled over the rock, planting pansies *(how perfect!)*. It is Cherry's beloved Barton. She watches him there on his knees, planting in the mud with such purpose. He is a fine-looking man, she has to give him that. As he delicately teases the tiny root balls from their plastic squares, she tries to picture him in that three-piecer he must have worn in his previous life on Wall Street. She thinks he looks pretty appetizing right now in his soggy wardrobe, standard-issue for the gay male: tight, shredded blue jeans; white t-shirt; and those army-issue, high-top boots.

Then Six comes running down the road and when she catches up to Barton, she throws her little body straight into him. Her daughter is shirtless and barefoot, with her wet hair hanging in her eyes. She looks like a wild Indian child, but Rae has no energy to scold her. *Wasn't it a royal waste of time anyway?*

Six waves to her mother and then hops onto the steel toes of Barton's boots. They dance an exaggerated waltz right there in the driveway, without reason or music. Rae watches Barton's distinct muscle masses shift under his wet t-shirt, which clings to him like ice on a lake. Then her eyes move down to the waist of his low-riding jeans and then to that tantalizing bulge below. He wears nothing beneath those jeans, she can easily tell.

It's so safe, she knows, this emerging crush of hers—he's gorgeous, but he's gay! *How one does long for what one cannot have.*

In his silliness here with Six, he bares for Rae his protective, yet playful side. Rae then realizes one advantage to living in this fishbowl neighborhood. Whatever shortcomings she and Sonny might exhibit in parenting can easily be filled by the cast of misfits in this park. She knows that Paul and Claude and maybe even Barton himself would have made better parents for Six. Watching him dance and laugh with her daughter, he certainly doesn't look gay, and might even be mistaken for her father to a stranger passing by. She knows that there are actual gay fathers and has no issue with that. She couldn't care less; who is she to judge?

Rae pulls a word search book and a pencil from the pocket of her robe, and feigns interest in finding the simple words buried in the jumble of letters on the page. She watches in silence until they finish their dancing. Six then scurries off to forage for food in the kitchen and Barton returns to his pansies and his soupy soil.

Rae loosens her robe and smokes one more cigarette. She climbs back into her trailer and brings out out a clean, white towel for Barton.

"I think you'll need this once you're finished. Looks lovely." She smiles as she bends low to hand him the towel. His eyes come up slowly and are confronted with the deep canyon between her breasts, which now are generously exposed by her open robe. Her index finger gently raises his chin and directs his eyes from her chest upward to her face.

"I mean you've done a really lovely job. I just love pansies." She says the words slowly and sweetly, as though speaking to a child—if ever she was to be that tender with a child.

Then she straightens up and turns on her bare heel, and all Barton is left with is the towel and the jumbled aroma of cigarettes, Chanel, and pheromones.

June 21

Walked with them again today. Some conversation this time. He is Paul. We discovered that we are both Michigan natives, did the obligatory showing of the mitten to point out our hometowns. Spoke of our common love for the lakes that are splattered all over the northern part of the state.

Again we sat for a bit. He assumed I might like to know something about his past. I gave him no encouragement but he persevered nonetheless. He had taken many classes in many disciplines while in Ann Arbor, courses in fine art, engineering, and Black studies, mostly Black poets. It was impossible to assemble them into anything as formal as a degree.

Then there was that little slot of time during which he would have politely listened to my academic highlights. I said nothing.

So he continued. He said he was as Detroit as the Tigers, Stroh's beer, and Vernors. Had spent many years as an engineer at GM, but not a single thing he designed was ever introduced to the car-buying public. Why they paid him over that time, and so generously, was to him a total enigma.

I spaced out for a few minutes. Watched the woman peel curls of wet sand out from under her toenails. When I tuned him in again he was saying something about returning the Corvette to its earlier, romantic design, with a masculine engine sheathed in soft, feminine contours. That line I liked. I mentioned my Airstream and he totally understood my attachment to it. No doubt about its gender, he said. Then he went on about the cars. I only remember bits...dash instrumentation bathed in blue light, like the light from a television in a darkened room...the psychological comfort of chrome...cars for people to fall in love with.

At the point when he started in about people needing to name their cars and lovingly bathe and wax them on Saturdays, I stood up, said I should be getting back. He said nobody understood him, that was why he left. Studied cooking instead. Mentioned their restaurant on the bluff in Orient. I must come by sometime.

I'll be sure to bring my month's wages.

She added nothing to the conversation. Before I left them I asked her name, and she turned toward me and offered her only spoken word, "Sloan." She held me in an uncomfortable silence, as though more was coming. Then he said she's his wife.

Six's compact frame lands smack into Rae's bosom. Rae pushes her away and holds her at arm's length, examining with wide eyes. The girl's waxy, black hair is plastered in thick mounds against her sweaty face and she lets loose her nonstop defense.

"Rae I had to sock him in the face if I didn't hurt him bad he would of come after me and he asked for it he did he shoved me Mama right into these fancy girls and they all jumped away like I was a disease and they were pointing and laughing at me so I got up and hit him as hard as I could right between his eye and his big ugly nose and then there was blood all over his face and everybody shut up and I ran all the way home and nobody came close to catching me."

A small, approving smile breaks on Sonny's lips, and when Rae sees it she pops him sharply on the side of the head. The school had already called. The news had awakened her.

She is exhausted, and speaks slowly to her daughter, more with bewilderment than anger. "It's the last day of school. Just one more day, that's all you had to do."

Rae's eyes look to the heavens. She hasn't had enough sleep. Again she focuses on her daughter and as she shakes her head like a metronome, she continues. "You are a complete mystery to me. Seems like you've been pissed off since the day you were born. You won't look twice at any schoolbooks and you carry 'round that sad little Bible like it was your sole protection in this sinful world. And if praying fails you, you beat the crap out of somebody."

Rae sits down at the kitchen table. She often feels like she's acting the role of mother; the everyday aspects of it do not come naturally to her. Still, she feels more confident in this little niche of parenthood—trauma management, discipline, damage control—all these she can do.

Six and Sonny sit with her and both relax a bit, relishing Rae's silence, hoping that the worst is over.

Rae lights a cigarette, and begins again with her first, long exhale, "I'm just too easy on you, that's all. Your father gives you no appropriate discipline when I'm out there working to put food on the table. He's got a girl of nine watching baseball 'til eleven on a school night and teaching her how to bait up and shoot a goddam rifle."

While Rae smokes, Six examines the hands in her lap. Sonny takes a moment to indulge in thoughts of his Winchester Model 70 Featherweight. Under seven pounds, the thing has the most gorgeous stock ever put on a factory rifle. It had been his father's. It isn't the firing of it that he loves so much, more the sexy feel of it in his hands—the warmth of the wood, the icy seriousness of the barrel. Yes, he had taught Six how to shoot it, but also how to polish and clean the rifle, and to respect its power. She never cowers when he fires at the row of Bud cans or rotting tomatoes lined up along the broken fence.

"Well, Rae, how many girls can stand in the shore-breakers and catch a bluefish for dinner? How many girls any age can handle a rifle?" Sonny smiles at Six, but his euphoria does not last.

"My point exactly. And *I* am the one to pick up the bullet-hole infested beer cans," Rae screams. "We are not white trash, even if we live in a trailer with cheesy painted rocks in our front yard!"

Then her eyes are fixed on Six. "All you're really aiming for is becoming an uneducated, pissed off, Bible-toting little *boy* with dirty feet and this knotty hair. I swear I'll drive you every single day to Greenport and set loose the nuns of Our Lady on you. You want religion? I'll show you goddam religion."

Sonny winces. "A girl has to protect herself, Rae. It's a mean world out there. Remember, Six didn't start the fight."

"But I'm ending it. Your father's going to drive you back to school, and you *will* apologize to that boy and do whatever ass-kissing the principal says you have to do to return to that school next September."

Rae twists her cigarette into the ashtray and returns to her bed in search of a deep, unconscious slumber. The truth is that all things parenting exhaust her.

Sonny and Six then dutifully pile into the Thunderbird, but drive directly to Rose's Blue Light.

"I'm not having you apologize to nobody," her father tells her. "I'll call your teacher later. You just stood up for yourself, that's all. Next time though, try words first. Can save a little bloodshed sometimes."

"Okay," Six says, and she watches her father drive slowly to the diner, lost in his thoughts. She knows he understands what it's like for her. And now she will be rightfully granted a pineapple milkshake for doing nothing but defending herself. *Praise the Lord!*

"I have no fresh pineapple, Sweets, so how about rhubarb? Trust me, it's incredible."

"Just chocolate, please," Six tells her.

"I'll bring you both, but believe me, the two of you are going to be fighting over the rhubarb milkshake."

Sonny and Six sit at their favorite table, the one closest to the jukebox. After his coffee and the milkshakes arrive, he slides Six a dollar bill to play some music. But before she even stands, the screen door slams against the plank siding of the restaurant. Rae's right hip is first to enter the diner. She looms large in every way and immediately fills the room to capacity. Even the cooks come out of the kitchen.

The enduring battle between Rose and Rae is legendary. There had been no affair, no fight, no known cause for the hostility. Generally thought is that the two women are like two black holes in space, both accustomed to pulling all matter and attention toward them. When they are in the same room, the static energy can force the flour out of your bread.

Now Rae stands in the middle of the diner, knuckles fused to hips. She assesses the situation. No one present can help but stare at her, the way her generous flesh is pumped into her v-neck, the excess bubbling forth making her breasts seem on the verge of attack. Her buttocks are tightly wrapped in spandex and a rump roast encased in cellophane can't help but come to mind. Not a word is spoken.

Then all eyes roll from Rae to Rose as she slams shut the cash register drawer. If the two women are going to go bosom to bosom, not a soul wants to miss a single spark.

Rae walks directly to her husband's table, lifts one edge, and sends the bitter extremes of ice cream and coffee into his lap. Six jumps to her feet, but soon finds her stiff little body plunked horizontally across her mother's hip. She offers no resistance to this humiliating position; she needs all her strength to keep the tears behind her eyes.

Rose flies from behind the counter and places her face directly in Rae's. In almost a whisper, she says, "You will clean up this mess."

All the money is still on Rae, who has the momentum of table-upheaval on her side.

"I'm not doing *shit*," Rae says. "You harbor this little truant one more time and I'll see to it that you're serving time instead of lousy hamburgers!" There is not currently, or has there ever been, anything as common as a hamburger on the Blue Light menu.

"You fire-engine-red bitch!" Rose screams in Rae's face. "Get out of my restaurant before I bounce you out on that blimp passin' for your ass."

The money now is on Rose.

Then Sonny courageously moves between them, facing Rae. "Listen, Babe, this is my fault. I should've taken her back to the school. Rose don't know anything about it. You take Six back to school and I'll clean up this mess, okay? Okay, Babe?"

Neither woman budges, their eyes lock right through Sonny. It is Rose who finally turns away, figuring that for once, she had gotten in the last word.

That never happens.

Rae places Six on her feet and sweetly tells her to wait outside, they'd be off to see Mrs. Solak shortly.

Once Six is safely away, Rae stands in the center of the diner and smiles as her face reddens. And then there emerges from the depth of her bowels the most fluid and sickening flatulence ever to hit the North Fork.

"And that, dear Rose, is the best thing on your menu," she says and proudly walks away from the feud and the mess.

June 24

We walked west on the beach today, thankfully in silence. A slow, meander-
ing pace. Paul rested his arm across my shoulder for a short while, like it
was the most natural thing to do. A whole world of vibrations and history
jolted me…what was it I felt? A poor, miserable childhood? A failing
marriage? His sexual ambiguity?

I grew accustomed to the weight of his arm and relaxed a bit. I was thinking
too much. My assumptions were based on nothing.

I like the smell of him, sweet yet astringent. He smells like spice, like clove
and cinnamon and a sweet vinegar. Like an entire meal. Probably like his
restaurant.

They are both so peculiar, so excessive; even her, excessive in her quietness, her
sharp angles, her fixed, glaring eyes like a trapped animal's. He is so frail,
more feminine than she, delicate, but possessing a beauty beyond hers, his
pale eyes like raw pecans, tapered at the edges, with heavy sensuous lids.
There is something exotic in his looks, a gentle nobility. His face, his color-
ing, his families, must all go way back. To northern Africa? To the
Caribbean?

Why am I so drawn to him?

But being around them feels a little unhealthy, as if they were a spicy ethnic
dish that tempts and shocks the palate, but later inflicts chaos upon the
entire digestive tract. But again I am thinking too much. Making too much
out of it.

"What a glorious morning!" she exclaims to the world.

Cherry emerges from her trailer promptly at 8:00 and performs what she calls her "routine maintenance." She works her way through a few basic yoga positions, pretzeling her slender but muscular limbs. These are followed by a course of sit-ups and then bicycling on her back with her legs airborne like two spinning Ferris wheels, her hands supporting her narrow hips.

She then takes overripened scraps from Sonny's garden and whips them with oatmeal and yogurt in the blender. This mush is applied as a mask to her freshly shaven face and twenty motionless minutes are spent in her chaise lounge. Then a cold rinse with the garden hose and into the trailer for the friendly burring again of the blender, mixing fruit, yogurt, wheat germ, brewer's yeast. A shower, careful selection of clothing, something creative with the hair, a thermos of coffee with cream is made and she's off on her bike to find Barton, most likely at his shed, to spend the latter part of the morning feigning interest in his work.

They don't make girls like that anymore.

FALL ASLEEP FORGETTING · 87

The sexy, tapered legs are still strong, but the top is nearly ruined. It is old; he can tell by the width of the boards and how it's joined.

When he'd first seen it, he knew he had to have it. This hadn't been a problem because it was free, discarded roadside on Shipyard Lane. Barton had lifted the table singlehandedly into the bed of his pick-up.

He continues his loving appraisal now that the table sits in the sun outside his workshop. Cherry had told him that this shed had been the only standing structure when her parents bought the land on the Sound. It is a simple board-and-batten, one-room building with a tin roof, two windows and a wide, swinging door. Inside, he has painted all but the floor an antique white, and has built a proper workbench. All his materials and tools are neatly stored, stacked, or hung.

He had known nothing about woodworking when he'd left the city. Through books, magazines, and the use of his growing cache of second-hand tools, he has educated himself methodically on all matters relating to wood. He has come to love the "masculine" birch and walnut for their strength and easy cutting, and the more "feminine" pine for its warm tones in aging and its workability. He has learned about coping saws, crosscut saws, keyhole saws, and then advanced to jack planes and mortise chisels. Vises and clamps became of particular interest to him, such as the old, wooden furniture clamps, and then three-way clamps that secure moldings to shelves or tabletops. Equally fascinating were handscrews and ratchet-type clamps that you can tighten with one hand. The more he learned, the more he wanted to know.

Now lining the workshop's shelves and window sills are jars and tins filled with nails, screws, washers, nuts, and bolts. He reserves Cherry's large, blue Noxzema jars for his prized collection of porcelain knobs. There are wood stains, putty, glue, and luxurious waxes and finishing oils.

Behind the shop beneath a makeshift roof, there lives a collection of things some might find useless, but to Barton possess great future value. A cast-iron tub is filled with chair and table legs, and a line of eel forks and broken clam rakes cling to the building's backside. There are wooden boxes of rusted hinges, door knobs, and drawer pulls. A broken rocker, ornate picture frames, and antique farm tools of a worn, intensely personal nature—these all are cherished by the woodworking novitiate for their intrinsic and historic worth.

There is nothing about the work he doesn't love, and loves nothing more than where he works...with the water behind him and the sweet perfume of pine everywhere. He labors bare-chested in jeans and workboots and prides himself on being a man doing a man's work, plain and simple.

Since embracing this new endeavor, Barton Ferris has earned $3,407 in furniture repair and the sale of his benches, side tables, and small cabinets. He maintains accurate records.

Barton now ascertains that this newly found table has been used most recently as a workbench. There are half moons of thick paint, swirls of old glue, and scars, pocks, and gouges. He fingers the deep grooves left by the base of a bench vise.

Then he leans hard into the table, his body advancing and retreating as he first scrapes and then hand-sands it. He wants to remove only the thinnest skin, being respectful of the table's past. He sees its surface as the face of an old woman, entitled to wrinkles and imperfections and more beautiful for them.

Barton empties his mind and labors only in his muscles, tissues, and jostled organs. He feels the steady, gentle pumping of his heart. His sweat trails from his neck, then falls away from his chest to the raw surface of the pine. This pleases him. Soon the only sounds are the wind easing through the upper limbs of the pines and the raspy shushing of sandpaper against wood.

Such is his perfect world until he hears a soft knock from below the table, at the top of his stroke. Barton stops, but hears nothing more. After his next stroke, he hears the gentle rap again. He quickens his strokes and a knock follows each at the same rate. *Shue. Tewk. Shue. Tewk. Shue. Tewk.*

He lowers his chest flat against the tabletop and shimmies to the other end. After craning his head downward, he finds the source of the noise. It is Rae.

She is on her side, her face cocked upward to his, only a foot or so away. Barton stares at her eyes, her perfect application of eye shadow, liner, and mascara. He strays to her lips, red and parted, and then, to her breasts, again partially exposed, pink and pinguid in the heat.

"Want some breakfast?" she asks.

He looks around. He is no fool…there is no food. "No, No. I'm…I'm fine." Silence. He turns his head.

"I need a tool," he announces. He carefully swings his legs off the table, stands, and hurries into his shed. Once safely inside, he prays she'll leave. He searches for some sort of shield or foil to protect him, and he settles on a long-handled chisel.

When he returns, she is gone.

Barton notices the impressive, wet imprint of his chest on the table's pulpy surface. She's left a white silk scarf on the ground, curled like a fallen flag of surrender. He picks it up and brings it to his nose. He abandons his confusion and smiles. He feels again like the successful financier he once was, vital and virile. He is still a man doing a man's work, a man tempted but firm in his commitment. With that thought to fortify him, he hides the scarf in the shed, and works and waits for Cherry to show up with his coffee and, hopefully, something to eat.

June 30

Spent most of the afternoon trying to forget the morning. Kept very busy, just routine, mindless caretaking in the sporadic rain. But after staring at my supper for the past hour, the whole thing is here in my face, humiliation upon humiliation.

The earliest part of the day, the sky had been dark and heavy, the sun hidden behind a dense, theatrical curtain of dark grays and deeper blues. Midmorning, we were back on the beach, the three of us, in what looked like twilight. It would rain soon.

We walked for an hour or so. The wind was constantly in our faces as we headed east, searching in silence for the missing sun. The air luscious, our skin dewy.

Finally we stopped and sat, facing the water. I was the closest to it, with husband and wife somewhere behind me. A new silence, a painful new silence, except for wind, water, and a distant grunting boat. Somehow deafening, this quiet. I closed my eyes. I thought of excuses to leave on my own.

But then Paul's hands came to rest on my back at some point, gently so as not to startle me. They did, but I didn't move. Slowly his hands spread up my back, beginning at the very base of my spine and fanning to my wing bones and shoulders. Then back down with his fingertips only. Then up with his thumbs in the narrow valleys along my spine, the effect of which I felt acutely in the soles of my feet. Down with his fingertips, dragging his nails lightly. Back up the rivers of the spine. Then rushing down, faster. And again. I dreaded he'd stop.

I can feel it now as clearly as then.

I don't know which of us brought these hands around my rib cage, who willed these hands along the natural upswing of the ribs to my breasts. Not in a rush, but in as natural a progression as time passing, or a spoon circling a bowl, or blood escaping from a small wound. Not startling, not wrong, but familiar. The warmth of his hands penetrated my breasts in his slow but forceful holding and releasing. His palms brushed roughly over my nipples again and again and I was lost in those hands, lost in the liquid air, a stranger in my own body.

I thought about his wife being there behind us, knew she must be watching. I felt even more excited by that. I thought this must be all right, within the definition of their relationship. I really didn't care.

His breath was thick on my neck, warmer and wetter than the sodden air between us. He drew his body nearer. I felt first the heat and then his form, more solid than I had anticipated. My mind threw questions I totally ignored, until my eyes opened.

Though these were strong, broad, unapologetic hands, they were also light-skinned and loosely feminine. They were her hands. I watched amazed, like watching a film, watched as they circled my breasts, as I allowed her palms to draw again across my nipples. Her mouth was on my neck. My mind was shooting commands, but my body was lagging behind, stuporous and content.

Seconds passed, or some increment of time, before I was able to lift my concrete hands from my sides. I grabbed her hands and shoved them into the sand on either side of me. I used that downward push to raise my own body.

I was on my feet. I turned to face her, and I'm sure I looked like a small, angry child confronting the wave that had just taken her sand castle out to sea. She wasn't looking up at me, but simply stared without expression at the place where my sand castle had been. Her hair was wet and plastered against her skull, from the air alone. And her arms, looking exaggerated in length and suppleness, lay dead at her sides, palms up.

Who was this woman?

My eyes found Paul. He was perched nearby on a swell of sand, wearing a very weak smile, a putrid tenderness in his eyes.

And then I did what any confused child would do. I ran away. I ran on and on, away from them, away from my confusion, heading nowhere, until the rain finally came and I threw myself into the Sound.

All I feel clearly now is shame. Not because I allowed her to touch me, because I did do that. And it's certainly not because she's married. He was in on this. What keeps bothering me is that I ran away like that.

They must be laughing.

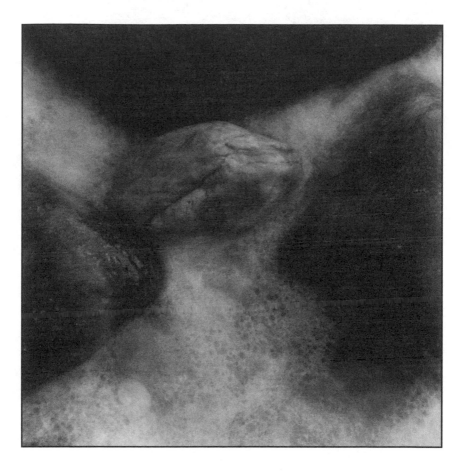

JULY 2001

I AM LOST IN THE IMAGE.
THAT IS THE BEAUTY OF THE PHOTOGRAPH.
IT HAS A LIFE THAT IS SEPARATE FROM MINE.

The basket is packed and the spilled coffee spreads over the linoleum floor in widening puddles. She stares at it as though it came from someone else's hands. The cottage is quiet now. The argument is nearly over.

"Let's just go for our walk."

"I don't feel like it now."

"I think we should, while my energy is still good."

"No, Paul. Not now."

"I thought this was decided."

"I've changed my mind."

"Do it for me, Sloan."

"Once you get something in your head…"

"You forget. It was your idea."

"It feels more like yours now."

Paul and Sloan appear again to Claude in their usual apparition-like way, coming from nowhere.

Sloan has a basket. Paul only carries a white towel. He motions with his eyes for Claude to follow along and like a harmless little puppy, she does, trotting behind them east into the low morning sun. The beach is a beautiful, odd mix of color—soft-pink sand, the Sound a harsh blue, and the evergreens on the fringe of the bluff an unnatural, neon green.

Paul leads, then Sloan, then their pet. This arrangement offers Claude an opportunity to study the contours of Sloan's body beneath her t-shirt and light, cotton shorts. Shoulders are broad and bony, a solid waistline, jutting hip structure. Nothing special, she thinks, but wonders, could this be the same woman who had touched her so self-assuredly? Best if the puppy just slogs along without questioning. But the pup can't help noticing the woman's scent…perspiration, soured wine, dreamlessness. *Had she slept in the clothes she's wearing?*

Claude tries to will her to turn around, to notice her. She dances in and out of the surf. She begins to hum without skill or melody. Feeling ignored, she comes up close behind them and pokes her finger into Sloan's basket. It is Paul who turns with a smile both nefarious and sweet and says, "Let's eat."

They sit right there in the cold sand while Sloan offers green olives stuffed with almonds, bread with sweet onions baked into the crust, smoked fish, and melon. It makes for a peculiar breakfast, but Claude finds she can't eat enough of it, as though saltiness and sweetness are all that matter in life. Or maybe, she thinks, it is just good food.

Once they are finished eating, they rest. Paul positions his body on his side in the sand and his wife places the back of her head in the curve of his hip. Eventually their eyes close as the sun really begins to heat up the morning air. All that food begins to dance maliciously in Claude's stomach. She stays awake and keeps a vigil over the tide changes and over the two of them. She watches the wind tease Sloan's t-shirt back and forth over her breasts and the way they lop in a lovely, full way, one atop the other. She wonders where all this is going and if she even cares.

But these are all lazy, aimless thoughts. It is just a fine, fine summer morning after a perfect meal in a perfect place with perfect strangers.

RELIGION IN THE HOME

HOW I LONG TO BE IN THE LORD'S TEMPLE.
WITH MY WHOLE BEING I SING FOR JOY
TO THE LIVING GOD.

Psalms 84:2

The night before, her father had cried out in agony at the same moment her mother had taken to prayer with a breathy "Oh my gahhhhhd!" Six had pulled out her Bible from beneath her pillow, and read out loud over and over her most comforting verse until she had heard the toilet flush for the second time. "The Lord is my shepherd: I want for nothing," she had prayed. "He makes me to lie in green pastures; He leads me to waters where I may rest; He restores my soul."

But now it is Sunday morning. Six is alone in the backyard where she has created a small sanctuary tucked behind her father's shed. There is a table with candles, her Bible, a few holy cards. She puts on her headphones and the oversized choir robe that Claude had found at the Op Shop for her. And with eyes closed and small palms cupped to the heavens, she tunes to WHYM and her beloved gospel program. She immediately begins to quiver and shake, and sings along loudly with the choir, unaware of her off-key squawkings.

"The! Love! Of! GOD!" The voices in the tabernacle are so lush and in praise so unified, to her it is as if everyone in the world is singing. Miles high over the piano flies the swelling beauty of their joined voices. She becomes one of the choir members and feels the beautiful light falling from the high windows touch her face with salvation's glory. *Alleluia!*

But then it is her mother's voice she hears bellowing above the choir. She turns and sees Rae standing near her with hands on hips and mouth opening and closing like a fish. Six can't make out the words exactly but gets the message. Why is it, she wonders, that her mother is always taking her from what she loves, to what she does not want to do. She nods in Rae's direction and, amazingly, this sends her away. This affords her a few minutes more to listen to Mahalia Jackson. Her powerful singing and the plinking piano send the girl twirling about in her robe like a crazed dervish. Then comes the guitar plucking and strumming behind the wailing voices of the Original Five Blind Boys of Alabama. When she hears them sing "alone and motherless ever since I was a child," it doesn't make her sad at all, but soothes her like a lullaby. She knows already that life is hard. She knows well that only God sees what is in our hearts, that only He knows what we suffer through. But all hope, everything you need, is clear to her in the song's words of praise and redemption—no matter how many troubles the Lord puts upon you, you will never be abandoned. Yes, she may have "one more river to cross," because we all do, but "change is gonna come."

She remembers the one Catholic mass she went to with her friend Arthur's family. She had found it boring, and spent the hour examining the stained-glass windows and the cozy little shrines on either side of the altar. For her, even though she liked the look and smell of the place, there just wasn't enough God in that church. The singing sounded like something people were forced to do.

Still, she knows that mass means a lot to Arthur. It is a comfort for the thin boy with the skin you can almost see through.

But here in her backyard church, Six feels miraculously transformed from a dirty-kneed girl of nine into a very powerful spiritual force in the world. And as her mother pulls her by the ear back indoors, she thinks about the saints pictured on the stack of holy cards she's collected. She can identify with those young saints especially, all so misunderstood as she is, all just suffering soldiers of God's will.

July 3

It all unfolded so inevitably, like a collision or a cold.

Sloan carried a basket. I walked next to her, staring at her. Who was this woman, so tall and angular? Her empty gray eyes were as inviting as a vacant parking lot. She does have lovely skin. I wanted to touch the downy hairs on her forearms. She totally ignored me.

It was hot. Our walk was long and we were well into our second hour. Paul found a kind of canyon, a secluded snip of sand protected by three massive boulders. There was a coolness trapped there, lingering from the night. We rested, or rather Paul rested. Sloan and I were still standing. We feigned great interest in little sand creatures and big cloud formations, trying very hard not to acknowledge what was screaming between us. I cannot express how strange it was, this concrete attraction that was a presence unto itself. I kept looking at Paul, but he was only watching his wife, expressionless, detached.

Whatever this thing was, it was flooding my own body.

I could tell she felt it too by her increased awkwardness and skittishness. The wind held her thin shirt tight against her chest and I could feel the blood warming in my veins. My body was becoming more and more a stranger to me. My skin, my eyes, the tips of every hair, probably my kidneys and gall bladder as well, all were magnetized and pulling toward her. My senses could not process all this data fast enough and I found myself once again staring at her.

I did notice that Paul was watching me, smiling just a bit. I should have questioned her motives, and his. Should have seen red flags, flashing lights, wooden arms lowering to block the tracks. I saw nothing, only the sun on her eyelashes, the perspiration on her upper lip, the way she looked down to me. I took in her smell. It was overpowering and I can't begin to describe it. It would be like describing the color blue to someone born blind.

Against my nature and habit, I went to her. I had to. As Paul watched with-out comment, I touched her. My hand dragged heavily through the air between us to fall on her cheek and around to the unbearably soft nape of her neck. With my other hand, I began to unbutton her shirt, as if I had done this many times.

Quickly but carefully I unwrapped her, using my hands and my mouth to touch the areas I uncovered. She was a cool, jelling liquid in my hands. Her weight fell against me, her vacant eyes closed. She was saying something, I couldn't make out what, but she kept repeating it, slurring the words together. These words could have been for Paul, but I took them as consent, even pleading. I lay her there in the sand and devoured her, mouthful by mouthful. It was more gluttony than lust. She let me do this without rejection or encouragement.

I was so much there with her that it felt like I was not. I brought her to orgasm in full view of her husband, in only a matter of minutes, in sexual territory I knew nothing about. Then she stopped her muttering and her shaking and released the palms that were pressed against my temples.

And just as abruptly I was back on earth. I could feel my soul returning to me, and my conscience, and an awareness of a bitter taste in my mouth.

But no time for all of that because Paul was breaking off chunks of bread to accompany the silver squares of hard cheese he had sliced. I saw there was melon cut and a bottle of wine uncorked. Sloan somehow was dressed again and already gnawing on a piece of bread. I had never undressed. I wasn't sure if what I thought I had just done had actually happened. My huge appetite was the only proof. Paul was chattering away about the wine. A local treasure, he called it, and went on about caring for soil and grapes grown without fungicides, balance in nature, and other gibberish.

These were the things, real and imagined, that we shared at around 11 this morning on a July day, in the absence of a single spoken word on my part.

Claude arrives at Sonny and Rae's to celebrate the Fourth of July. Six is about to light the sparklers she has placed in little cups of sand on her backyard altar.

Claude takes the matches from the child's hands and lights a sparkler. "Hey, you've got a real Yankee Doodle religious experience happening here," she says.

Six dismisses the comment. "There's gonna be fireworks on the beach tonight. You coming with us?"

"I might climb up on top of my trailer to watch them," Claude lies. She dislikes the excesses of this holiday, especially the loud, showy, unnatural displays in the night's sky.

Sonny has made corn tortillas filled with jack cheese, jalapeño peppers, and shreds of chicken, all swimming in a thick, tomato gravy. There's yellow rice and a dense salad of avocado, red onion, tomato, cilantro, and a fresh white cheese.

"My sauce is inspired by my passion for my wife," Sonny explains to Claude. "When I gently squeeze the ripe, voluptuous tomatoes into the pan, she always comes to mind." Rae rolls her eyes and Sonny laughs and continues, "Then I add my own secret ingredients, which might be something like beer, cumin, tabasco peppers, a little onion, and something to cut the heat, a kiss of cinnamon. And there you have it—Rae in a pan, hot and sweet."

And with that observation, Rae sidles over to her husband and whispers something in his ear. Sonny smiles, pumps up his chest, and grabs another beer. "Not too many, love, at least until I go to work," she says. "Tonight is a night you might want to remember."

Claude helps Sonny move the patio table and chairs out under the stars, and they place candles all around the yard. Sonny puts on some Latin music and Rae begins to sway with its sensuous rhythms. She takes the hands of her daughter and channels the undulations into her small body. They continue to dance on the dusty earthen floor until Sonny and Claude begin to bring food to the table.

"I wanna sit by Claude," Six announces.

It's nearly dark once the four sit down to eat. A timid breeze manages to keep the mosquitoes at bay but the candles still lit. Sonny spends the first few minutes of the meal just watching Rae enjoy what he's piled on her plate. Her taste buds are like sensitive electrodes that trigger a world of responses from her body: humming and giggling, pats and rubs for the lips and belly. There are already splats of sauce on the front of her white halter top. "You're going to get these out, right?" she asks him, pointing at her bosom. Sonny smiles and nods.

Once they are finished, Rae presses her full, separated lips on her husband's, and mingles his flavors with her own. This time, everyone hears her whisper to him, "You cook like you make love, my sweet, with a charming disrespect for recipe." She kisses him once more. The golden skin of his face bronzes, and Six groans as she begins clearing the table.

Claude is touched by Rae's rare show of sentiment, cloaked though it is in constant sexual innuendo. Unfortunately, this thought provokes in Claude's mind the vivid image of Sloan's naked body sprawled out on the sand. Claude runs her fingers over her sore knees, still tender from friction with the sand. She feels confused; everything seems familiar and yet foreign to her, from the rituals of the dinner down to the rumblings in her body. She suddenly feels out of place, accompanied by a rising heat in the throat. She too formally excuses herself to help Six with the dishes.

Later, she is alone on the beach, watching the last trails of fireworks disappear into the darkness. "If I'm going to survive this summer," she says to herself, "I'd better stick with plain and simple food."

July 6

I must write this down or it will be one more dream, one more thing that never happened.

They came for me again this morning. I was at the park well before 6. They were there not long after that. How they knew I'd be there that early is a mystery. Or maybe they weren't looking for me at all.

We walked in silence in a neat little line right at the water's edge. I remember the tickle of the water between my toes, the warmth of the sun already, and feeling a little trapped with Sloan in front of me and Paul behind.

We stopped walking. Without asking, Paul undressed me. He did this slowly and with such care, actually folding my ragged shorts. Our eyes met a couple times. Sloan undressed as well, and then Paul stepped away. The world at that moment was spinning way too fast and then somehow I was on my back, the sand beneath me molded to the contours of my body. I could feel the earth's pulse on the underside of my knees. Sloan stood above me, at my feet, naked, with the rising sun shrieking pop-art tones of red and orange behind her, leaving her body's interior space a deathly blue. I swear then that I felt removed from it all, as though we were frozen in a flat painting I was admiring.

I looked around and found Paul safely curled into a bluff to my right. His eyes were open but his body seemed asleep. He stared at the sea. Then I checked to see if any other human beings were around. I guess the rest of the world was occupied elsewhere.

I stared at her still form again. I tried to make her an inanimate object. I thought of photographing her in black and white, and then storing her in an orange box under my bed. There was the wide pelvis, usually balanced by her broad shoulders, but expansive from this angle. A small but tangible pot in her belly. High above, breasts dwarfed and dangling and unthreatening, almost laughable. Her long nose stretched close to her chin and her hair flew around her face like errant petals of a sunflower lost in the wind.

Then for one moment, or possibly much longer, her eyes, her face, her very being focused on me with such intense detachment that I couldn't resist being pulled into her, magnetized by her presence, by her past, her marriage, pulled into all of her and all her lost dreams.

The tides had turned. She had beaten me at my own game. There on that bed of sand in that fraction of time was insignificant naked me and the whole of her beautiful, tragic, sad life. Or this is how I imagined her past to be, the thing that seems to make her disappear into herself.

She lowered her body and she placed it on mine. A million molecules on my skin's surface came alive and I was lost in the sum of her parts. All those things I had so harshly judged became her greatest weapons. I saw Paul close his eyes. I felt her inside me. She was rough and unapologetic. She braced my back to control the rhythm of my response. My body was limp, so lost, letting her take whatever was left of me, praying that the thick ache would end soon. And it did.

I cannot be the first woman she's been with.

Finished with me, she dressed. Paul brought my clothes to me. Then she took her husband's hand and walked with him back along the water's edge, to home, I suppose. She might have just finished a morning swim by the look of her relaxed gait, feeling no regret for abruptly leaving the embraces of the sea. But not me. I felt as if I had witnessed a horrible accident and had just watched the ambulance pull away, feeling intensely drawn into others' lives and then left alone in the shrieking, silent aftermath with absolutely no idea what would happen next.

July 8

Now the hours seem long, the hours I don't see them, don't see her. This second day dragged on and on. Repetitive tasks. Everything annoyed me. Some fool carved "Jude is gay" into one of the picnic tables. Did they mean Claude? Am I? Have I always been? Is it even something you have to either be or not be? I haven't changed my sexual orientation because of my attraction to one female. I have not overnight become a lesbian. That noun, lesbian, sounds more like a member of a political party or an alien, such as a Libertarian or a Martian. If I were inclined to make a habit of this, I would prefer to be called gay, a harmless, happy adjective. But I am not.

But is she? What about him?

I doubt that this is just some kinky sport for them, that he gets turned on by watching his wife have sex with a woman. He's too serious, it's all too serious, almost ritualistic, with the seductive sharing of food, the long silences. The way he stands aside, as if to condone, even bless what we do.

I don't know her one bit, even like her at all, or desire to. I can imagine loving Paul. But desire him? No. Combined, I suppose they would be the perfect lover.

Then again, there might be no more of this craziness.

Descartes wrote that we are moral to the extent that we control our passions by our reason. I have a great respect and need for reason. There is no reason for this passion. Is there reason to control it?

I am not so far into this thing that I can't step away.

Except that I think about her constantly, about her body, her breath, her silhouette against the sunrise, the colors that I now associate with her, intense colors, all the oranges and reds and that unnatural yellow of her hair. I wish I could paint them away.

God, let them be there in the morning.

ART AND MASON JARS

It's late, well past midnight. Three beer bottles line the countertop and Claude holds a fourth, half empty, in her left hand. She sits at the small table in her trailer in the melancholy light of a single lamp. Before her is something beyond the AM/FM radio and Mason jars her grandmother left for her in this trailer the day she died. It is what Claude loves best, more even than the photographs of people she can't identify, more than the old, musty quilt.

Most cherished is this book, entitled *Modern Painting*, which was printed in Lausanne, Switzerland in 1953. She runs her hand over the blue cloth cover and the red gothic letters, engraving its title like the inscription on a tombstone. The spine is broken, and when Claude opens to the first page, she fingers the failed, golden glue. She sticks her nose into the book and unearths the subtle tones of her grandmother's scent, something like Lily of the Valley meets Pledge furniture polish. Page one has liberated itself and bears the name *Fada Claude Lambert* scripted in black ink and underlined on the upper right. She touches the middle name and then flips to the very last page and reads what she has read so many times, written in the same flawless script: *Sometimes one must use a heavy metal object to unclog the laundry chute.*

She has no patience for her journal tonight. Tonight she will visit Cézanne's *L'Estaque: The Village and the Sea*. This image always brings to mind her own curving Main Road and snippets of the village of Orient. The painting comes alive in her soggy, dreamy head with the movement in the trees and the crops—she can almost see them growing—and the playful sea in the distance.

Claude turns then to possessed portraits by Munch and the dreamlike sensibility of Chagall in *Self-Portrait with Seven Fingers*. She flips to De Chirico for his cerebral muscularity and then to Klee as a comfort food. She shares a fifth beer with Kandinsky on the heady, romantic battlefield of *Composition, 1914*.

But once she sees the bared breast in Matisse's *Red Odalisque* with all the reds and yellows and oranges, and after she spends too much time on the woman's closed eyes and voluptuous indifference, she angrily closes the book.

Claude decides not to drink the one remaining beer in her refrigerator. She returns to the last page of *Modern Painting* where she finds the three letters she has read so many times. These are letters written by her father to his mother. There may have been more, of course, but these are the only ones Fada had saved. In each, he describes a girl with an odd name, a curious misfit at five, at ten, and finally at seventeen. They contain other small details of her father's work, vague comments about Claude's mother. But her father writes in striking specificity about his only daughter's dark beauty, her trouble at making friends, her hiding for hours in her closet. "She is so bright and fascinating, but I may be the only person who realizes this," he writes in his last letter. "She dresses in the plainest clothes, reads constantly, and I fear shares her thoughts and ambitions only with me."

She puts the letters and the book away. She thinks about her grandmother as she drifts toward a hopefully numbing sleep. She wonders why she bequeathed this trailer to her. *Was it meant to be her closet on wheels? Was it only because they shared a name, or did her grandmother sense something in Claude that mimicked her own reticent, renegade spirit?*

She is left only to dream about the many gifts she's received from a woman she had never met.

July 10

Finally, they showed up. It was late afternoon, threatening rain. The beach was empty. We walked only a short distance.

She was just ahead of me. I reached for her and pulled her back against me. I tightened my arms around her, closed my eyes. A blanket appeared. She turned and we were at each other, half-dressed, messy, abrupt. Neither of us came. Just frantic, fast elevations, over and over. It was like shoveling food in your mouth but never swallowing. Even Paul looked confused by our wheel-spinning and when she pulled away and began dressing, we looked at each other and then both of us at her.

Her head poked out of her t-shirt. I saw her neon blonde hair captured by the wind and illuminated strand by strand by the lowering sun. As she turned to look at me, her hair slashed brutally over her eyes. Looking into the vast depth of grays of those eyes is like looking out a window at a morning thick with mist. Everything in weak detail, but felt more intensely through the abstraction. In that brief look, I saw her yielding, which was a little heart-breaking to witness. She lowered her head and looked for her sandals.

Before I'd finished dressing again they were walking away from me. His questions, her answers not for me to hear.

She follows me like a ghost, a shadow, or a bad dream. I close my eyes now. She is still here in this room. I can see every feature of her face so clearly. The pale mismatched eyes, the elongated off-center nose, broad forehead offset below by a knot of chin, randomly drawn eyebrows, lashes in the varied colors of sand, full lips curling in winding lost directions, the hair like random haystacks on a scorched field. Too many details. Enough.

She is homely. Can't speak.

I just brought home a man I barely know. We had an awkward twenty minutes in the pull-down bed and now he's sleeping there. I had hoped it would clear her away. It did not.

"What is this thing?" Six flips the contraption back and forth in her hands.

"It's a light meter. It reads the amount of light available so you know where to set the camera's shutter speed and the aperture."

"Don't need this with Sonny's camera. Just open the cover and it does all that stuff on its own," Six says, spinning the dial skeptically. "I'm hungry."

Claude knows she looks a mess, hair uncombed, eyes red and burning from lack of sleep. And she knows she should get back to work, but instead she lifts a stack of work prints. "Come over here and tell me what you think of these. In a bit I'll make you some corncakes with a truly gross amount of maple syrup."

As Six gets up and walks to her, Claude sees how much alike they look, both so boyish. And although Claude's breasts are large for her frame, her hips—like Six's—are narrow and poorly defined. Their hair is dark, cut fairly short, without discipline or much style. Six's face, however, is all her own, a concoction of Rae's mysterious eyes and bone structure with her father's rich skin color. This is a face that will take some growing into, Claude thinks.

Claude is pleased that the child is so at home in the Airstream, as much in her environment as she is outdoors. She is always in motion in the wild, though here she lies low, pensive and quiet. The trailer's intimate confines and Claude's books and stacks of prints encourage this. Six loves the disappearing bed, which now hangs open, unmade from last night. Six's stellar collection of beach finds, including starfish, fish vertebrae, fishing lures, and the actual jawbone of a muskrat is secreted away in a wooden box beneath the eating table. There are used books Claude has purchased for her at Lenny's in Greenport—Bible stories and books on Indian legends, bugs, and tropical fish. Six is free to come and go as she pleases, and even free to stay the night, providing Sonny knows where she is.

The child now wedges herself between Claude's lap and the table. Still facing forward, she brings her arms, thin and so dark, back around Claude's neck. Print by print, they examine the mysteries revealed in

Claude's time exposures, how they form unexpected shapes and colors and make solid things semitransparent.

"Was Jesus a white man? The Bible doesn't say," Six asks out of the blue. She keeps her eyes on a photograph that is very dark and somber.

"What?"

"He didn't have dark skin like mine, I bet."

"I don't think it matters what color his skin was."

"I heard somebody call Sloan a nigger lover."

"Now, who could that be, I wonder."

Six's face darkens. "He's an idiot. He doesn't know Paul at all. He hates everybody. He'll go to hell for that."

"Hold on there, honey. I don't think your God works that way, do you? You're right though, Saugerties doesn't know Paul. Sloan knows him and loves him for who he is, not what color his skin is, and..." Claude drifts unwillingly into the lumpish muddle of that thought. After a short silence, Six turns to her and says, "And?"

"And what?"

"And what am I? My skin is even darker than Paul's!"

"My understanding is that you are part Native American and part Mexican, and whatever your mom is, maybe German or possibly from Venus? Hasn't your father talked to you about this?"

"He told me I come from a long line of Lakota warriors. Lakotas are Indians. But Rae says I'm turning as black as the tires on her Mustang. That's why maybe part of me is like Paul."

"And that's a bad thing? I'm not sure what Paul's heritage is, but he's probably some exotic blend from Africa and the Caribbean. You may be darker than he is, but that's not bad. Hey, the best chocolate is the darkest."

And with that last bit of wisdom, Claude crosses the time limit imposed by nine-year-olds on heavy matters such as this.

"So I like these pictures okay." Six neatens the pile and pushes it away.

"They're yours if you want them."

"Yeah, sure. Are you gonna make those corncakes now?"

"Yes, I am. Hey, did Solak pass you?"

"Yeah, she did. She had to or she'd have me again next year. She told my mom that was scarier than my report card."

"Nice work, my little truant. So, let's celebrate. Go swipe some strawberries from Cherry's garden, will you?"

"Or I could just ask her."

"You're right, my honest friend. That would be the respectable thing to do."

July 11

*I went to them today. I sought her out. I found them behind their cottage
and interrupted their breakfast. I tried to coax her into the cottage,
but Paul insisted, right there. It was over quickly. Sex as convenience store.
Paul seemed more interested in playing with his bowl of fruit.*

*Who cares if I know nothing about her, if she has a favorite color or some
dark pain. I'd rather know that slit of light below her veiny lids and the
flutter of her eyelashes and the way her eyes roll upward when she climaxes.*

That's all I need.

Any feeling beyond lust that I have for her is more pity than affection.

I'm not looking for love and a life and dishes that match. I have a life.

f32

There on the secluded beach with boulders left and right towering above her, Claude performs repeated acts of great intimacy. That is an intimate connection with her camera and this sensuous, swirling moment in time.

Everything is in motion. The surf is insistent, reckless, and unpredictable. She witnesses the sun's intensity reflected in small clippings of the seawater around her. She stands in a shallow pool and you can already see the tides' movements by the salt markings on her rolled-up trousers. The wind travels through her hair strand by strand. And the light is so rich that she can feel the seeping weight of it in every pore. She will strip away the light's color and force the black and white film to render images more dreamlike, more poetic. Poetry, she knows, is not language adorned, but language pared down to the essential, as these natural elements will be transformed into a concise visual exploration of turmoil or tranquility or transcendence.

It's difficult for her to stabilize the legs of the tripod on the curved, wet surfaces of the rocks and in the shifting sand, especially given the heavy, nodding head of the camera. Finally, she feels the camera will hold steady through the many exposures over time.

Then Claude's fingertips move gracefully around the body of the Mamiya. To her, it is a simple machine, practical like early farm machinery. There is no light meter within it or auto anything. From her external meter she reads the light reflecting from a gray card, f16 at 125th of a second. Breaks it down to the eight exposures she'll utilize to create the single image. Sets the camera at f32 at 1/500th.

She pops open the viewfinder, loving that snap of attention as it reveals there, extracted from the physical world, a square of light. The vivid color is distracting to her. She must look beyond that color and focus on the structure of the image, which will be revealed in the myriad grays, blacks, and clean whites. That is the muscular power of the black and white composition—there is no fat.

She releases the shutter. Cocks it again. Waits. Remembers. Feels. Releases. She constructs a new image, layer upon layer, not like an artist but an artisan. Then she winds the camera's cranking arm to advance the film. Again, more watching, more waiting.

July 13

a stack of color images, imperfect things

follow the water's movements, let the elements emerge and disperse, be a stranger to them

pure vision is transference, of light, of thought, of memory

absorb color, saturate the retina, look through the image to the rag pulp, feel the paper as a tangible, honest, simple vehicle

follow the rhythms in the image, free the forms of their content, let color and light and line be enough

bypass the mind, all just reactionary emotional mush, clogged with too many memories and high school math, get rid of all that

I could throw away all these prints. Would I be a different person without them? Photographs are relics of the past, no matter how much art is muscled into their creation

I dreamt about her, about them last night. We are in a cellar. I smell rotting fruit, but it is a sweet, churchlike scent. There is very little light. I see their faces as floating ovals, bodiless. She has a photograph in her hand. They won't let me see it. Wordlessly, they taunt me. Finally she turns it towards me. They are hysterical when I ask who it is. She laughs without sound. The photograph is of a woman walking away. It is you, Paul tells me.

Personal truths and values are often documented on a person's refrigerator. You might think that Claude would tape a few of her photographs on her small fridge, but there are none of those. They are taped and stacked elsewhere. This is what you find on the bright-white surface:

a black-and-white photograph of an thin, old woman with a long nose, sitting in an aluminum chair in front of this very trailer (Claude found this picture in a galley drawer);

a snapshot of Six standing proud and bare-chested next to her bike;

two film processing pick-up slips;

this poem, poet unknown, on tattered newsprint:

> *It's not that I'm so grand*
> *I am not*
> *but am more than less awake*
> *and not*
> *sleepwalking among the anxious,*
> *dreamless crowd,*
> *idling collecting,*
> *possession proud*
>
> *I see obesity in modernity*
> *I see no place in it for me*
>
> *Not a preacher*
> *not so grand*
> *secondhand is what I am*
> *slightly used, irregular, soiled,*
> *mismatched, worn and driven,*
> *lived in, recycled, without*
> *prestige or proven value,*
> *boring as bread*
>
> *Not a preacher*
> *not so grand*
> *a simpleton is*
> *what I am*

July 14

I crave her. Here is my weakness. There is never enough of her. I always want more…more of her body and more often. I crave the pure, uncut, pharmaceutical-quality sex and the high it renders. There is never enough.

I've become self-indulgent, greedy. I covet.

For all my brown rice and secondhand clothes, I am in my own way on my cell phone, eating a cheeseburger, driving my SUV straight to hell.

A TICKLE OF SWEAT

A tickle of sweat, curving under her breast, wakes her. As slow and tender as a lover's fingertip, the bead travels the substantial distance with pinball accuracy, then joins earlier drops on the sheet beneath her. It is about three o'clock on a brutally hot afternoon.

There is glorious, dead quiet. She can feel the sunlight as it passes through the pink chiffon cafe curtains. Like a caress, the light comes to rest on her exposed thigh and there delights in that creamy expanse. Rae's eyes open in a series of dainty blinks.

She rolls from her side to her back. There is no hurrying to be done. It is Saturday and fully July. Even the dense humidity seems to have a comfort to it, as long as she doesn't exert herself, which is exactly her plan for the remainder of the day.

Her darling Sonny has placed a thermos of iced coffee—laced with cream and vanilla, the way she loves it—on the nightstand. She has only to reach ever so slightly to bring it to her. Sonny and Six are probably marketing as is their habit on Saturdays. Dinner will be lively and fresh, she is assured of that. *Saturday, the juicy, ripe peach of the week.* Maybe even lobster, she's been that good, at least as far as he knows, she sniggers. They are probably already in Peconic, snagging Rae's favorite Chardonnay at the vineyard with the field of young sunflowers.

Rae unscrews the top from the thermos and slugs the brew directly. The ice bouncing playfully against her upper lip inspires her to lower the container and place it between her thighs. It is shockingly pleasing, the delicious cold. She changes positions to relive the sensation. Then the sheets come off and her nakedness becomes a plump, pink sofa in a tiny room of a shabby Parisian brothel. She feels nothing but exotic, especially so in this land of potato fields and tourists. What was that bumper sticker she'd seen? Something like, *If it's tourist season, why can't we shoot them?*

There and such she lies for some time in the heat, feeling the icy coffee course through her, perfecting in her mind a glorious blank. Rae has that little technique down pat; fifteen years in the ER has necessitated it. At this moment she is all body.

But once fully immersed in her body, she unearths deep aches in her calves, soreness in her ankles, and a sharp pain in the small of the back. *On her feet the entire shift!* Then Rae remembers the mammoth, drunken fool they'd scraped from the floor and hoisted to the gurney. "Time to pamper this body," she says.

She rises from the nest of sheets. *Just a plump, lovely chicken,* she surmises, as she catches her image in the full-length mirror screwed to the backside of her bedroom door. She fluffs the wildness back into her hair, and runs her fingertips down her chest and over her hips. She is large, but firm, a full-course meal of a woman, she assesses. *Fine dining in a world of snack food!* She smiles at the woman in the mirror; she is all the more alluring for the sexy sleepiness in her eyes. "C'mon, you hot, juicy thing, let me cool you down some," she says, and barks a laugh from the back of her throat.

Rae sashays down the narrow hall to her bathroom. There she collects the filthy remnants of Six's wardrobe from the floor and deposits them into the wicker hamper, already overflowing, but not her concern. She quickly scrubs down the tub. A fresh towel. Water on and with plenty of heat. She louvers the high window wide open. Then with a flip of the radio switch comes all that her little heaven lacks…James Brown. Well, he just drives her wild with the primal urgency of his rhythms, the way he chews up lyrics and spits them out as a pure aching beat. "Baby, baby, baby. Baby, baby, baby, I got the feelin'."

She sings with her man as she steps into her tub. There she stands, motionless, like a Brooklyn Madonna in her used tire. She piously waits for the water to cool to a tolerable temperature. "You don't know wha ch'you do to me," James tells her. She feels the dissipation, cell by cell, of her solid mass into liquid, into the dense air and the delicate water rising to her calves. Then she eases into the tub. A mere babe she feels, enticed back into amniotic fluid. Once on her back, Rae watches her buoyant breasts become shining islands of paradise. A slow smile comes to her as she more accurately tags them islands of *captivity* for so many lost men. "Give it up turnit a loose!" James affirms.

This is signature Rae. Who can say why she is a powerhouse of a body magnet, but even the tub water is drawn to her, getting funky on a molecular level, turned on and energized, slopping over onto the tiles.

Rae shuts her eyes and she finds the underbelly of James's groove—the bass and the percussion. Oh, she gets his message... *sex is a mind-blowing drug and you don't need to be a nurse to understand that!*

Her eyes open to find that the intense late afternoon sun has forced its way through the cloud cover. It transforms the high, tiny window at the foot of the tub into a high-intensity light source that shoots directly at her. She lowers her lids, and as her eyes adjust, she makes out the silhouette of a head in the window. It can't be Sonny, she thinks; he'd need a couple twelve-packs and blind ambition to reach that window. And this is not his moppy head of hair; this mass is brushed neatly to one side, with some nice height and fullness. Then she knows.

She throws her arms open to the sides of the tub like a prizefighter disrobing. Then she raises her body a bit, allowing the bath water to run in rivulets from her breasts and belly. And then, just to flex the pain in Barton's groin a quarter-notch more, Rae drops her knees to each side of the tub's rim.

She smiles at him demurely and says, just loud enough to be heard over the music, "Take that, love." And then, still smiling, "you horny, mixed-up, little bastard."

July 17

Her orgasms are violent eruptions. No emotion, just plain unloading. Even when she takes me there, I feel her emptiness. She could be pulling weeds. Her mind missing in action.

I see now that equal parts repulsion and attraction make for the most voracious form of lust.

July 19

In an open field, I heard movement above me, a long rush of air. I looked up. There were hundreds of small, black birds traveling in wide waves. They made a paintbrush swath across the sky and then came to rest, all of them, in the trees and wires that ringed the field to the north. Then on one unspoken command, they all took flight again and traveled en masse overhead, dipping and diving, for the sheer pleasure of flight and companionship.

We are different. We destroy pleasure by overanalyzing it. Seems impossible for me to just enjoy the sensation. Does it always have to mean something?

She thinks hard about what to wear, especially which scarf will be perfect. Which one will be light enough to carry the wind and trail behind her without falling to her back? It must be brilliant in hue as the colors on the beach are so drab and muted. She will stand in dramatic contrast, vibrant in her dark distress.

Tongues were waggin'. There are no secrets in Cherry Grove!

Cherry selects a simple but classic, peach-colored summer dress. She wraps her head in a long, flowing scarf of rose and the same peach on a background composed of all the colors of parchment. She crosses it beneath her chin and leaves the ends free to fly when she will walk westward into the sunset. All right, she thinks, it is a little over-the-top Norma Desmond, but it is how she truly feels. She slips on her dainty sandals. *A gift from the infidel!*

Picking up steam, she slams the trailer door behind her. Something made of glass shatters. She prays it belongs to him.

She wonders if he's looking out the window, watching her take her first steps in leaving him. Because she surely will, rather than see him fall all over himself in front of that mountain of flesh. She doesn't get the attraction, but she can smell it on him. Rae flirts with him, yes, she thinks, but then she comes on to everyone. She's probably worked her way through the hospital's entire staff of physicians and has taken on the orderlies for dessert! And now, Cherry realizes, Rae is so desperate that she is seducing a gay man. *But he doesn't really love her. How could he?*

She finds herself already at the beach. Her scarf catches on an offending hemlock, and she unfemininely frees it, yanking with both hands and tearing the fabric. Cherry tries to run in the sand, but then stops abruptly. Lifting each foot with a ballerina's grace, she removes her sandals and flips them into the beach grass. She may regret that later, she realizes, and takes note of the location. She slips off the scarf as well and drops it; it's just an Op Shop find anyway. Maybe the original owner will pick it up and value it again. Without knowing why, this thought brings on real tears. She keeps walking. She doesn't and does want a living soul to see her like this. She is far from being defeated, *it's just that...*

Barton Ferris is the one unlike all the others. Those Manhattan men, she recalls, were like spawning salmon. She never felt a thing for a single one of them.

But then she'd seen Barton in his fine, pinstripe suit and starched, white shirt. His sandy hair had been just a little too long, in his eyes and just over his shirt collar. The night he had walked into Luchow's was the very day he had left Goldman Sachs. Just walked away from all the ambitions that had never been his own. Cherry and Barton had been together that night and every night following. He simply took up residence on East 9th Street, never bringing more with him than the clothes he had worn that night and the black leather briefcase that contained papers on his investments. He had assured her that there was money enough to carry them well into the future. *My God*, he had looks, *and money*, and a husky boyishness that would win any girl over.

Now, she thinks as she walks more slowly into the splashy sunset, Rae Gutierrez is wrecking her perfect world. Had they stayed in the East Village, she would have worried about the constant enticements; but out here in Nowheresville, the place is crawling only with dykes, farmers, and fishermen! She thought he would be safe here. *Had he changed?*

She swings her arms and moves her legs with a limp grace and pronounced sadness; it is the gait of a person with an uncertain destination. Then she stops, pauses, turns, and storms off in the opposite direction. She and Rae have much in common, she realizes. Both of them are profoundly feminine, sensual, sexual. Of course, he'd be attracted to them both. And if she lacks Rae's confidence and cockiness, she vows right then that she will fake it. *This is war!*

July 21

They touch often, while walking or eating. They create an energy field that to me is impenetrable. Even when I'm intimate with her, I am on the outside. I cannot explain this any better than that.

The unspoken rule seems to be that he is always with us.

He seems to be growing less interested each time.

This morning on the beach, after everything, she sat apart from us, her back to us. She faced the water, motionless, her unruly sun-bleached tangle of hair sat atop her bare back. She resembled an abstract sculpture composed of hay and bronze.

I wanted to go to her, to lay my hands on her shoulders. Comfort her. Reach her in some way. But that might be misread as affection. Affection is not allowed. So I just sat there with Paul and we watched her. We both honored the wall she had built around her.

He told me then that that's just the way she is. That she's content enough inside her world. He said this without looking at me, his eyes still fixed on her. And then he rattled off the sad, sad tale of their meeting and early days together.

THE CURVING SUPPORT OF FEATHER PILLOWS

FOR WHATEVER WE LOSE(LIKE A YOU OR A ME)
IT'S ALWAYS OURSELVES WE FIND IN THE SEA

E. E. Cummings

"I thought she was mute when I first came across her at a public library...in Hamtrammack of all places. She said nothing to my pleasantries as she checked out my books. Ignored all my small talk and just turned her back to me and walked away. I followed her into the stacks where she was shelving. I watched her for the longest time." Paul is staring at his wife's back, examining her sturdy chain of vertebrae as she sits there by the water.

"I've never understood why she started talking to me, because now I know it's so unlike her. She probably caught me staring at her. I didn't want to frighten her. I cautiously stepped closer to her, not too close, and I asked her something innocuous...if she liked working there. I thought it would be a great job, I said, being surrounded by books. But she said that she hated it there, that the books tormented her because she never reads. She might just as well be selling men's underwear." He smiles.

"She never reads?" Claude says, there at his side, toes in the sand, with arms crossed over her chest.

"She whispered to me that she couldn't read. She said she could read the words, she knew what they meant, each one of them. 'But when I get to the end of a paragraph, even a sentence,' she told me, 'I just can't put them together to mean anything.'" He is silent for a few moments. Claude is ready to leave them at this point, to get back to the booth or anything else. But she stays on.

"For the first six months we spent together, I did nothing really but read to her, late into the night. Mostly children's stories at first, *Winnie the Pooh* and *The Jungle Book,* and then slowly we moved into Hemingway and Carson McCullers. One night I brought a few of my poems...I write just for myself, you know. It's not high art. But I never read any of them to her, even though some of them were now *about* her. It seemed too personal, just too heavy, too soon.

"So I read these books to her late into the night. Ate horrible take-out food. Never cooked anything ourselves. And every night, I drove back to Ann Arbor through the nearly deserted streets, going over the evening in my head."

And then a longer silence, painfully long to Claude. How can she walk away now? She wants to. She thinks of an excuse that seems believable. She begins to get up, but his hand gently pulls her down. He goes on.

"We sat on a maroon velvet sofa with two bed pillows. They had blue ticking covers, yellowed they were and without pillowcases. I wondered if they were pillows from her childhood. I never asked her, of course. Again, too personal. I really never asked her anything or confided to her any of my own past. Not then. I was very content to sit near her. I loved looking at her, liked her messy hair and long, perfect nose, her cockeyed frown when she sat there, listening and concentrating. Sometimes she'd ask me to reread whole chapters and I would. It didn't matter to me what words were coming out of my mouth. And I relished that random zap of..."

Paul turns to Claude at this point and with a sense of shared intimacy that confuses her, he continues, "...that zap of something that we all long for. Not merely sexual electricity, but emotional electricity as well. I had this drug-like high around her."

His eyes leave Claude and settle on his wife again. "It was like nothing that had happened in my life before was really all that important. None of it was relevant to my reading to her, on that wonderful couch in that dark apartment, the curving support of those feather pillows on our spines and necks." Another small smile.

"There was no physical relationship, maybe a forkful of food delivered to the other's mouth, the most innocent of caresses when meeting, a single stroke on the back. Simple signs of uncomplicated affection. It was all so innocent, as if we were children, free to explore the companionship of another person without the confusion of sex and adult complications. Do you know what I mean?"

No answer.

"We spent almost every night of the week together in this way. She brought the books home from the library. I have no idea why she picked the ones she did. But one night, I was reading from a book we both really enjoyed, a collection of poems by e. e. cummings. She liked him a lot and found his fractured style easy to get. That condensed language was actually perfect for her mind. I remember one by cummings, a wonderful poem about Maggie and the sea. We sat there for a bit, just soaking in this beautiful poem, and just out-of-the-blue she took me by the hand and brought me to her dark, dark bedroom, where I, of course, had never been, and there on her too narrow bed by the light of a single candle..."

"I get it," Claude says.

"By the light of that candle, all hell broke loose. Or maybe, more accurately, she broke loose. We never slept until the sun was long up, and we had made love in nearly every room of that apartment, even the kitchen. And God, the tub.

"Claude, I had never felt these things for a woman before, and that was the way I felt about her from the moment I saw her. Maybe it was the way she needed me. And, of course, her looks. I had a huge curiosity about the world within those sad eyes."

His wife stands then. She might or might not have heard her husband's tale, but seems to sense its completion. Alone, she begins walking back toward home, hands in pockets, head down. Claude and Paul follow silently behind her, walking in step, lost in separate thoughts.

July 22

*Ours is not the mystical lovemaking they shared in the single bed and God,
the tub. His sad little fairy tale stirs in me a mix of jealousy and curiosity.*

*Why did he confide the details of their meeting, their lovemaking, even
her...what are they? Disabilities? What is wrong with Sloan? Does he
want me to feel compassion for her?*

One more thing. I think he is sick.

She climbs the bluff and enters the restaurant. She needs to talk to Paul. The books, the pillows, the single bed have been haunting her, both in her dreams through the night and the more pungent, fleeting images that have darkened her thoughts all day.

Claude stands in the entranceway. Her eyes are stunned by the intensity of the low sun, and the details of the space only gradually emerge, as if in a tray of developer. She is shocked by the seeping visual; it is like suddenly seeing a naked woman, spreading her palms to cover what she can from your eyes, so vulnerable, so enticing. She rubs her eyes to clear away all the dreamlike details. Then she looks again. The space is now a stark, black-and-white image, punctuated with hand coloring—the dull greens of wine bottles and the elaborate flowers on each table.

Her eyes are drawn to the high windows and the sumptuous light that lilts down to the tables in their white linen shrouds. These tables are lined up straight as pews along the side walls and are dotted with white dinner plates. Something in her suggests that she should genuflect. She resists.

Claude walks slowly into the room. The flowers are resplendent against the neutral setting—bending spears of veronica, lavender, and delphinium. Soft, overripe petals of roses create splats of color on the table linen. There are common wildflowers, tails of variegated ivy trailing almost to the floor, and shocks of ornamental grasses. Claude finds it all excessive but beautiful.

She senses a complex odor in the room, beyond food and flowers. It reminds her of a musty wooden church, with undertones of incense and overripe fruit and spilled wine. It is a dense and acrid smell, but not unpleasant.

Then Claude sees the photographs. Some are whole images and many are torn in pieces. All are crudely adhered to the white brick walls. At first, she doesn't recognize them as her own in this odd setting. But it is her seawater lapping against the hard walls, penetrating the bricks, disappearing into them, trying to escape. She runs her fingers through her hair again and again as she walks from image to image.

She feels violated. These are who she is, these black-and-white and color prints. These massed exposures of the seashore, very close up and intimate—the wending water, the fluid edges of rocks, the restless sand—these are all the familiar objects that define her obsessive style, her admittedly obsessive nature. And now she sees herself exposed on every wall in these grouped or overlapping or single acts of thievery.

She has never exhibited these personal documents; they were never intended for that. These may as well be pages from her journal plastered on these walls. She has never sold a single print, but has given many away, to Six, or to Cherry as barter, or to anyone who had shown an interest in them. She's left them behind for people to come upon, and in the trash for Barton to collect. To see them like this, dismembered and plastered on the walls, is unbearable.

Paul appears at the far end of the restaurant. He pauses near a table and rests his fingertips there. Claude's eyes find him and then stray to the food and drink that is now making its way from the kitchen to a large serving table. She watches it accumulate there, the charred and bloody meat, breads, cheeses, melons, more wine bottles.

Then with the poise of a monk, Paul walks straight to Claude, his arms rising in apology as he draws near. He places his palms on her shoulders and locks his eyes with hers.

"Are you angry?" he asks. "They need to be seen, you know. What's the good of keeping them hidden away?"

Claude pulls back and looks around the room again. "You never asked. They're mutilated." Anger clogs her throat. She walks away from him, and then around the room quickly. Her eyes move from one memory fragment to the next. She runs her hands over the photographs.

"They came to me this way, Claude. Some were in pieces," Paul calls to her. "Six brought them to me, a few at a time. And then Cherry, she brought some. I mean, you know, they're really wonderful. We started taping them up. It was just a novelty at first. But soon…they began to bring life to these walls. I never really wanted anything on them, but we all thought they seemed so at home here."

Claude turns toward him. "All? You all thought what? Some of these are just test prints, *discards!*" she shouts.

"And I *like* that…that they're rough and honest," Paul shot back, "and finished and whole or not. We worked very hard. We wanted them to look random but logical. Six loved it. She was so insightful. She…we all did…took the whole thing very seriously.

"Gluing them down and coating them with acrylic, Sloan did that. Claude, believe me, we did think about this."

Claude examines a large print, one that had pleased her, and she remembers giving it to Six. It was a favorite spot of theirs, and the image had the child's sense of exuberance and playfulness. Small stones and bits of shell danced in the moving water. Now she sees the strokes of the brushed-on acrylic, thinks of Sloan's hand moving over her image. She wonders if anyone has thought about how these photographs will decay beneath the acrylic? At some point, they will all be yellowed and brittle, worthless.

Paul moves closer. "Come to my kitchen and I'll feed you," he says. "The kitchen is the best place to eat here. Cherry's coming by soon. She's always a great distraction." He stops. "Of course, I'll remove the photographs if you want me to." A pause. "They are your possessions."

Possessions. The word reverberates in Claude's head. It is petty and naive of her to think this way given what *he* has shared. She knows that's what he's really saying.

Claude turns and walks away from him. In four long strides she reaches the nearest wall. The fingers of both her hands go to the bricks. Palms flat, she closes her eyes and feels their coarse texture and then the silky surface of a print. She digs an edge free and sends a strip of the paper screaming from wall to floor. The ripping is a hard, amplified sound and it soothes her, like an angry child feeding on the power of her own tantrum.

She's laughing now. But the sounds are like ugly, brittle shards of glass scattering across marble. The laughing comes in spasms with more sheering of paper from the wall.

After a couple dozen scraps of the prints have fallen to the floor, Claude pulls a chair from its perfect placement at table and sits there. She's quiet now, calmer, and she stares at the eastern high windows.

She wants to scream at him, to transfer to him all the anger and confusion she feels. But the pressure in her head has eased and the anger seems to be dissipating. She lowers her eyes away from the light and looks once more at him. The elegant man in the long khaki shorts and African-print shirt has left the room, taking with him his arguments, his justifications, his impatience with her. Now, in his place, stands a frail, hollow-cheeked man, still proud and full of pith and vinegar, but so tired he is struggling just to keep himself upright.

Paul sits down and lowers his head. She comes to his side and with one knee to the floor admits, "I could eat something."

At that moment comes another shrieking laugh and it startles them both to their feet.

After her hysterical spasm passes, Cherry says in mock seriousness to the two, "I have a few things I'd like to tell you, Father, once you've absolved my little friend." Then just a chortle, and while she tightens her sarong about her, she twirls and takes in the mess on the floor.

"Uh-oh. I guess somebody doesn't like our little exhibition."

Cherry then walks around the open space and picks up pieces of the photographs. More food is being brought out from the kitchen and once Cherry reaches the buffet table, she begins pointing. "I'll take some of that lovely smoked fish…and those potatoes there…and a few slices of melon. No wine tonight. Tends to make me suspicious."

Paul smiles. "Claude, help her package it up. For the two of them, you know. They prefer to eat at home. And take what you like as well."

Paul and Claude are now face to face and of equal height as his eyes again lock with hers. "What's mine is yours, " he says in a lover's whisper.

July 24

A small portrait.

Six is challenging the waves. She throws her tiny frame into the surf and rides for free to shore. Now she shakes the sand from the bottom of her suit and in a single stroke, rakes her hair away from her face. Again she fearlessly attacks the sea. And then again.

I feel protective. I'm not the maternal type but I feel an aching weakness in my knees for her safety. She seems so small and the sea so capable of spinal damage or at least a broken finger. But I am here.

She just threw me a wave and a come-join-me fluttering from the wrist. I raised my notebook and pencil in weak excuse and motioned for her to go ahead, brazen down all the waves that tower over you.

July 26

It was around 11:00. I found Sloan tending her herb bed in a steady rain. Crowds of comfrey and sage and a purple-leafed basil surrounded her. I stood and watched her from a short distance. She didn't look up.

The constant rain all morning made staying at the booth unnecessary. Any fisherman willing to brave the storm deserved free entrance, so I went out walking and found myself there. I haven't seen either of them in days, not since the fiasco at the restaurant.

Maybe I've been granted what I asked for, release from them.

Her gardens have an overgrown, tangled look, with odd combinations in a maze of packed raised beds. The rain made everything waxy and vibrant, and the diffused light was ideal for rendering color, luscious even in folds and shadows. Scarlet runner beans, deep-red dahlias, liatris, eggplant, and the velvety gloom of black hollyhocks. More somber plants than I can remember now. Purples, black-greens, and saturated reds. A new palette to associate with her. A disturbing yet alluring, mournful canvas of what Sloan sees as beautiful. Rising from these subdued hues emerged buoyant colors as well. Floating just above and within this dark sea were bits of white and orange and yellow from nicotiana, roses, agastache, and the weirdest of all perennials, the flaming torches of kniphofia. This garden must be the source for the restaurant's flowers.

She half-smiled and nodded when she finally did notice me. As I approached she reached into her apron and offered me pruners. Handed me a rusty trowel. She smelled of thyme and peppermint.

Around noon, the sky did brighten. The rain didn't stop but each drop became smaller, lighter, and more playful in the mild breezes. I was working with the tomatoes, pinching off suckers, tying and restaking. I picked a tomato that was especially ripe and felt the warmth of the fruit in my hand. It was as if the very act of growing was throwing off heat. I felt the tautness of its thin skin and the pulsating meat beneath. I bit into it and the fruit felt alive in my mouth. I remember bringing my hands to my stomach thinking I would feel it pulsing and moving inside me. I sat down on the edge of the raised bed and let the rain rinse the juice and seeds from my face. It took awhile.

While recovering from my psychedelic tomato experience, the light changed again. The sun came out fully, but the swaying particles of mist remained. Everything was bright but ghosted in grays, neutralizing the blue spruce and the ancient white cottage. The sky itself was metallically flaked, creating a surreal, infrared depiction of moisture in suspension. It was truly magical.

I closed my eyes to better see it and store it all away. I felt the wet caress of the mist as it laid its hands on my face. Smelled the piquant musk of wet soil. Droplet by droplet, the downy mist wore away my resistance and I felt lighter and happier than I have in a long time.

The wind then gathered its focus and pushed in a serious cloud mass and the rain returned. Grays deepened to dark blues and it mimicked the magic hour between day and night, a lovely twilight. I continued working, moving from the tomatoes to uprighting lima plants that had been leveled by the rain. I found a white, porcelain-enameled bucket and filled it with green beans.

Then I saw her on her knees picking blueberries in a patch east of the cottage. She combed the branches with her open hand. Her hair was a darker blonde and flattened against her head, making her forehead protrude, her nose seem longer, her cheekbones bulge.

I watched her work. I felt a new pull toward her, not because she looked beautiful there in the rain, concentrating on her blueberries. She simply looked familiar, and I found her for the very first time to be a comfortable presence.

She walked toward the house, motioned for me to follow. I follow well.

Paul was nowhere to be seen. Was he sleeping or at the restaurant? Maybe hiding in the next room? He would be disappointed if he was. I felt absolutely no desire for her. This new familiarity numbed all that.

We went to a screened-in room off the side of the cottage. There were heavy branches of evergreens above and I liked the sound of their brushing against the roof. There was a wooden table with a lit oil lamp, an old rocker, some *shells placed with care on the frame ledges of the screens. She removed for me my camp jacket, heavy with the rain and the smell of it. She has undressed me completely before, but this felt like the first tender thing she'd done.*

She brought me a towel, a dry shirt, and then slices of peach, bread with butter, and after that, a small bowl of aromatic, clear clam chowder, and some musky white wine that tasted a little off. We drank it from the bottle. I sat on a daybed with noisy springs with her sitting across from me. We said nothing until I said lamely that I really liked the food. Thank you. So formal, so polite, so much more I could have said. She cleared away the dishes with her head lowered, which on another person might seem like shyness. On her I knew it signaled retreat. As I grabbed my wet jacket, I caught her looking at me. She said my name and I thought more was coming. But that was it, and she went back to her gardens and I made my escape, as instructed.

I remember all these things as they happened or as I imagine they happened. Much of it was so very dreamlike. Memory is always part fiction.

Somehow she has solidified. She is not a caricature or a demon. She is just a woman, estranged from a world she feels no part of. She is a recluse. Her only connection to this planet seems to be Paul and her dark, magical garden. And through her one extraordinary tool. Her intensely sexual nature.

Claude is an odd name. Too many feeble vowels. The words it resembles are not nice words, things like clod and clot and clawed. I've never really liked it. Today it's a man's name. As it's my runaway grandmother's middle name, I associate it with the hermit's life that I inherited with her Airstream. Claude. It's always seemed more verb than noun. It means "to carve a life within one's self."

Sloan spoke that word, my name. All she said, but it was a mouthful. She exhaled it, excised it, and when I think of that sound now, I like it, this name. She rounded it, smoothed it, blew it up to noun status.

She arrives at the booth as the sun is rising; the force of her antici-pation had made more sleep impossible. Her cup of black coffee is now a swirling, burning pool in her stomach.

She's not sure if they will come. She and Sloan had been alone, for hours, without Paul. That may have broken some agreement unknown to her.

And then they are in the distance, as vague as a memory coming slow-ly into recollection. She sees his arm draped over her shoulder. Sloan carries a blanket and a basket. Closer yet and they are talking in tones that may be whispers. And laughing Claude thinks, because she can see their bodies vibrating. Or it could be the rising heat.

They take Claude with them without any more invitation than pass-ing by her so closely. She hurries ahead of them, leads them to the pine grove. She sits there, her back straight against a sappy tree, and waits for them to catch up.

Paul arrives from behind her. He runs his hand gently over her hair. His touch could be a breeze, it is that soft. Still, it startles her. Sloan kneels in the pine needles and produces from the basket white ceramic plates. She piles on them thickly cut bread, a very pungent, soft cheese, and a pile of black-purple jam.

Claude takes her plate and places it in her lap. She stares at the messy presentation. Sloan has not looked in her direction even once. Paul begins to sketch abstractly on the surface of his plate with a shred of the bread dipped in jam.

An erratic brittle current courses through Claude's body, from the soles of her feet through the congestion in her groin to the muddle in her head. Paul senses her agitation but says nothing. He eats nothing.

Claude forces down a fistful of bread and the clot chugs down her throat and into her knotted stomach. She feels everything too much, her shallow breathing, the intense humidity, the buzzing between her ears.

But Sloan has no trouble eating; her appetite is huge. She breaks off chunks of the bread with her long, dirt-rimmed nails. Her hands are like mechanical claws on a lanky crane, hovering over the bread and the cheese and the jam, lowering, grabbing, raising to her mouth. She eats with her whole body, jaw hacking away, arms protectively encircling her plate. Her monkey feet are bouncing and twitching in the bed of needles beneath her. She stares at her food as she eats, like a liberated captive might his first real meal. Repulsed, Claude looks away.

Paul still eats nothing, just sips from a plastic bottle of spring water. Again and again the bottle comes to his lips, but the water level seems never to diminish. He watches the sea roll in and out, peering through a narrow break in the pines. Then, while massaging his kneecaps, he looks at his beloved, shoveling food in her face like a peasant. He smiles at her.

Finally, Sloan stops eating; there is nothing left on her plate. She does seem to have trouble swallowing the last mouthful; her eyes bulge out as she forces it down. Then she reaches into the basket and extracts a half-filled bottle of wine. It looks to Claude like the questionable wine from the screened-in room. Sloan rips off the cork with her teeth and takes three or four hard, full hits. With a broad palm she smacks the cork back on and drops the wine bottle back into the basket. No invitation is made to Paul or to Claude.

Sloan's eyes return to Paul and he summons up another diluted smile. When she finally turns toward Claude and her lapful of food, it is Claude who feels embarrassed. Sloan turns away and then she belches, a rumbling eruption that seems to take everyone by surprise. It is low-moaning and aromatic, this gurgling, and once she has expelled it, she rises to her feet and extends her hand to Claude.

She yanks her up too quickly. Claude's plate and all its contents fall to the ground. Once standing, she is almost eye to eye with Sloan, and that is when Claude kisses her. Her hands cup Sloan's head and she holds her lips on hers. Sloan does not pull away; her eyes close and her hands dangle at her sides. Claude stays there and tastes the awful wine, the jam, and what might be the bitter remains of troublesome dreams. Then Claude is the one who walks away.

She barely has the strength to make it back. She lies her body on the floor of her booth on a worn, woolen blanket. She examines the texture and subtleties of the uneven grays and greens of the fabric. She then dreams of a rainy afternoon at sea, full of wind and uncertainty. She sleeps for hours rolling on the crests and hollows of desire and illusion, allowing time to pass at will.

AUGUST 2001

A FLOOD OF LIGHT
RELEASED FROM DARKNESS
ONLY TO BE CAPTURED IN THE SOUL

A FINGER IN THE PUDDIN'

WHEN IT SNOWS IN NEW YORK CITY,
IT'S LIKE PUTTING A WHITE WEDDING GOWN
ON A PROSTITUTE. SHE LOOKS PURE AND SWEET,
BUT SHE'S THE SAME FEISTY WENCH SHE ALWAYS WAS.

Stephan Kazmierczak

As is their habit, Cherry and Claude meet at the Blue Light for an early dinner on the first evening of the month for the purpose of payment of rent. They saunter into Rose's looking *tout à fait* the typical couple, but with a twist. Cherry this evening is in a slinky skirt riding well above her knees. It is a flashy red, set off by a crisp, white, sleeveless blouse. Her blouse tails are tied in a knot just above her exposed navel. Cherry wears red heels and her hair is piled high on her head. Her makeup is appropriate for early evening, plenty of color but applied with a light touch. The overall look she achieves is a little Glenn Miller, a little Elly May, with just an intriguing hint of streetwalker.

Claude's hair is combed back away from her face, held in place by the humidity and also with something that smells to Cherry like olive oil. Claude wears clean if not pressed khaki trousers and a white Oxford shirt with an unbuttoned, button-down collar. Black zoris and a dab of rosemary oil behind each ear complete her presentation.

"Why, Claude, you smell good enough to eat, if I went in for your sort of cuisine," Cherry says. Claude smiles and with an exaggerated sweep of the arm, leads Cherry to her favorite booth, the one with good road exposure. Claude sets her orange Agfa box next to her. The box as always contains two prints, offered to Cherry as barter for a portion of the rent on Claude's slip at the trailer park.

Before looking at the prints, Cherry tucks her bag away and crosses her legs. "You'd think Rose could come up with something better than this vinyl to sit on. It's like Velcro on the back of my thighs."

She takes the box of prints and sets it in front of her. "You know, when I lived in the East Village, I would just be rising around this time of day. I worked nights, you know, at this drag queen restaurant where straight folks could come and ogle the queers. After that, we'd all play the rest of the night away, until daybreak usually. The last hours before dawn, oh that is when the city really comes alive, when all the queens and their subjects dance and fornicate. This was long ago, b.b., before Barton. I would wake the next afternoon, usually around four, to the smells of summer before I even opened my eyes, because, sweet Claude, it was the aromas of the East Village lofting through my garden apartment window that would wake me. That scrumptious mingling of scents! Dals and curries, espresso, garlic, and baking bread! A sensual alarm clock, if you will."

Rose now appears at their table. "I'll just bring you what I know you want. Save a little time."

"That'll be just fine, Rose," Claude says. "Hold the meat, though."

"I'll let that one go," Rose calls out as she walks back to the kitchen.

"Me, too!" Cherry chimes.

After the prints are viewed and appraised, Cherry's face takes on a mock seriousness. But it is Claude who says, "Could you just keep these for yourself and not hand them off to Paul?"

Claude looks so earnest and self-righteous, Cherry has to smile. "What's mine is mine, or so I thought. But, as you wish."

They both watch a parade of ferry traffic pass. "Why do we have to be the strip of toilet paper that connects Cornecticut with the ass end of Long Island?" Cherry complains. "I hate all this traffic!"

Before the mood darkens further, Rose arrives with the seared tuna dressed in crusty herbs and sesame seeds, the roasted potatoes and fennel, and a diced tomato and parsley salad. The two eat in silence as their discontent is worn away mouthful by mouthful. At meal's end, Cherry places her fork gently on her plate and looks at Claude.

"Aren't we having a good summer, Peaches?"

The look on Claude's face surprises Cherry. It's not that Claude looks about to cry or break down, but rather that she has the blankest, most pathetic look on her face. She is a lost child on the midway of the state fair. Cherry decides to keep it light.

"I hear we are having a good summer. An eyewitness, the name I won't divulge, has told me so. And I'm not a bit surprised—I mean look at what you're wearing! Who am I to call a dyke a dyke? Of course, how could I be in any way judgmental of the whole thing?"

Claude watches traffic now moving eastward to the next ferry.

"I've always found them a quirky but interesting couple and you're alone way too much. And way too serious," Cherry continues without much of an audience. "She is quite lovely, too, in an exotic, caged-animal kind of way." Then she whispers through a wide, knowing smile, "And you know, my girlfriend, that a finger in the puddin' is perfectly okay if the chef doesn't mind you doing it."

"Cherry, please."

"Well, anyway, keep an eye on him for me, lover girl. He does not look well. I worry for him, and for *her*, of course! As long as I've known them, she's never said more than two words to me, or anyone else as far as I know. I fear she's, you know…"

"Retarded? A little crazy? She's not," Claude says.

"Oh, are we a little protective? That's understandable, one does tend to excuse lumps in one's own puddin'. I do with my own sweet Barton, more than I should, no doubt. No mind, back to Paul. My regrettably well-educated guess is he's got AIDS. But don't get me wrong, I've been HIV-positive myself for over ten years, although I've never been really sick. I take my meds and have assumed a very healthy lifestyle. Barton's negative and I will keep him that way.

"But, my Paul. He is the second sweetest man I've ever met and I've never known a soul more passionately committed to food! And to feeding *me*! Once the dear man intentionally burned my lamb chops just so Barton would believe I had actually cooked them. It must have pained Paul so to do that."

Her smile vanishes then. "But he is sick. I can smell it on him. Ask Rae. Maybe she's seen him in one of those dreary clinics at the hospital. I actually asked him about it last week. Asked him if he wasn't feeling well. 'Problems with my digestive track,' he said. 'Maybe a bug.' Bug, my ass. If he's hiding it, it's probably AIDS."

She doesn't remember hitting him, only sees the blood on his beautiful face. The bag with his dinner from Rose's sits unopened on the table. He is on his knees in front of her. Her first response is a natural protectiveness. *Who has done this to him? Has she?*

Then she remembers that her poisonous jealousy had brought her to this, the jealousy that now keeps her frozen in place and unwilling to help him. *She had confronted him, that's right.* He never lies, that is his problem, so sinfully honest he is. Had stammered on about Rae's flirtatiousness, how she was always coming on to him, that nothing had happened. He is just a man, he had said. *That was his defense?* She had corrected him, "You are just a *gay* man. *My* man!" And then she sees it, the horrible thing playing out in her mind, like a scene from a soap opera. Her eyes had bulged unattractively and she had started flailing her arms, punching at his face with power but without precision. *She had kicked him, hadn't she?* And her anger had only mounted when he offered no resistance; he just limply took it all. It had infuriated her. With the same passion—and for the same reason—with which she makes love to him, she had beaten him. *She had.*

He gets to his feet then, shaky at first, teetering from side to side. He shakes his head and blood flies from his face. *Oh sweet Lord, his face.* It is all too real for her now. Cherry reaches for him, goes to him with every cell in her body. But Barton raises his hand and stops her. He steadies himself and turns away. He slowly opens the flimsy screen door and vanishes into the August night.

And there she stands, alone with the overturned chair, the red-streaked floor, her pitiful, useless remorse. She's done it now, she knows. More than just losing the man, she's lost the battle, the war, everything. The defeat she endures at that moment is more than she can bear.

So she tries blaming Barton. *He'd left her, hadn't he?* He had been unfaithful, if not in actions, certainly in his desires. Cherry knows that is really how you begin to leave someone—in your head. *That bastard!* She tries very hard to want to strike him again, to reconstruct that anger, but she fails. She has never hit a living thing in her life, not a dog, not even her hideous father. Then she remembers the brutish way she had answered the slurs in high school. *But that was self-defense!* Now she realizes that she has hurt the very person in the world she loves most.

She wanders into their bedroom, lies on their bed, puts her face into his pillow. She does not cry, but chooses to pray to a God she has no choice but to believe in. Not being a violent person, certainly not a bad person, she begs forgiveness from that stranger in the heavens. If God sends him back to her, she will never strike him again, she promises. She will make it up to him, somehow make it all right.

And only then does she cry herself to sleep.

Six knows that extreme weather can actually *make* things happen. How she knows this, she can't say. Perhaps the knowledge comes from her father or maybe she was just born with it. Later, once she's seen what happened to Barton, she will chide herself for not having paid attention. She might have figured it all out ahead of time. She might have warned Barton and saved him from harm.

All that day it had been breathlessly hot and humid. Sonny had set up an aluminum tub of cool water outside for her. As she sat there, the sun had looked to her like a bright yellow beachball as it sailed in slow motion across a weird, too blue sky. A definite warning sign she had missed.

And then around dinner time, all that heat had fallen hard to the earth's surface. The sky became an empty gray shoebox that Six had felt was placed over them all, keeping them trapped by the humidity and the cardboard sky. No air, no escape. Things always start to happen when people feel confined like that. She remembered Rae saying that folks get pushed past proper by that kind of heat and humidity. Six knows that what might happen on a night like this would never happen on a day when tiny bits of snow dance in the sky.

Now tonight, Barton appears at the edge of their property and even in the weak light Rae can see the blood on his face and in his hair. She sits outside with a magazine and a pack of cigarettes, some Chablis. She had taken the night off, and had been doubly disappointed that she could only find this lousy box of wine in the cupboard and that her husband had passed out hours ago. So here she is in her aluminum chair in a sticky, feeble breeze that smells to her of mold. She walks slowly to Barton and takes his hand, as though he were a lost child, and brings him to the light of the trailer door. Rae cocks his head this way and that. His shirt is plastered to his skin with sweat and she pulls it up to assess the extent of his injuries. When she heads inside for a wet cloth, peroxide, and bandages, she finds Six with her face pushed against the window screen. Rae takes her by the shoulders and directs her back to bed. "There's nothing here for a kid to see," she tells her as she pulls the sheet to her daughter's chin.

"Is he okay, Mama?" Six whispers.

"He'll be just fine. Probably messed himself up with one of his silly tools."

Once Rae is back outside and arranging her supplies on the tabletop, she asks, "Was it Cherry? Of course it was. Over *me*?"

He is silent for a minute and seems again that sad little boy to Rae. Then while she cleans him up, he explains, "I'm stronger, but I would never hit her back. She had to fight her way through school, you know. She had to. They never gave her a second's rest."

"Well, she did a job on you, love," Rae says. "You're pretty bruised up. It's tender here, isn't it?" And then she runs her fingertips across his rib cage in a less-than-professional manner. "You know, it seems a shame to be punished for a crime you haven't yet committed."

• || •

Later, it is the low-moaning thunder and the heavy rain that wake Six, but it is the repetitious, drumbeat grunting from below that confuses her. She thinks it sounds like somebody is digging down there, groaning with the lifting of each shovelful. She is too tired to worry about it and drifts off again, comforted by her father's throaty snoring in the next room.

But beneath the mobile home, her mother lies on her back with mud oozing between her cheeks, loving Barton's force and weak little kisses. She is also laughing in her head as she pictures the two of them in the light of day. You'd see a woman naked, caked in mud, and a man bandaged and drenched in remorse. As she envisions this, Barton comes with one final exhale and she kicks herself for not having been sufficiently present to collect her own orgasm.

They gather their clothes, which cannot be worn, and crawl back out into civilization. The only light now comes from the kitchen window, but it is adequate enough for her to find the discarded condom wrapper and a blanket from the back seat of her car. She covers herself with

the blanket and then scurries inside for wet cloths, towels, and something for him to wear. Once they are somewhat presentable, she brings
him to the red couch and tucks him in under a cotton throw barely
big enough to cover him. A motherly kiss on his forehead, and she is
off to the shower. Soon she is snuggling with her oblivious husband,
comforted by his familiar sounds and smells, with the lovely rain outside cleansing away the crime scene.

But for Barton, sleep will be but a pretense for hours. His eyes are
stinging and his entire body aches. *He must never tell her.* To do so would
only be selfish. Now he and Rae have finished their business. It is
Cherry, and his life with her, that he loves. He is sure of all this. As
the washing machine dutifully hums in the background, he realizes
that one must sometimes commit the sin in order to be free of it.

As Sonny looks at the young man sprawled on his couch, he knows that his wife has betrayed him once again. She has even dressed him in *his* boxers. But Sonny lacks the energy or the passion at that moment to explode at the all too familiar, so he goes to the coffee-maker and begins his morning ritual.

"Why is Barton sleeping on our couch?" Six asks in a sleepy voice that is husky for a child. "Why is he dirty and beat up?"

"How about I make scrambled eggs and bacon for you, daughter, and when Barton wakes up, we will ask him."

As he prepares their breakfast, Sonny thinks about Cherry. He pities her more than himself and realizes that her jealousy will become some huge, airborne thing that will hover over them all, like bad weather. They'll all be dragged into their personal crisis, thanks to Rae. Here lies the poor, tortured faggot who loves a woman who is really a man, but has a fling with a woman who is more like most men Sonny knows— cheating, vulgar, hard as roofing nails. It would all be laughable if it didn't involve his wife.

At this moment, Rae lies half asleep in their bedroom, with the top sheet tight between her legs. She is flipping through random images of the boy...those delicate wrinkles at the corners of his eyes, fine and pale against the deep bronze of his skin. His classic handsomeness. Why, she wonders, is this type of look so often on *gay* men? Models and actors and athletes. *Well, he isn't that gay, now is he?* Here she feels a blush of pride in her own formidable sexual prowess.

Her mission at this point is the usual damage control. Sonny will need soothing. He'll figure it out, probably has already. She'd left a trail as subtle as a porn film. But how could he feel threatened? *This is not some-one she's likely to run off with.* As for her part, she must refrain from indulging in leisurely thoughts of Barton, will not dwell on his hard angles and protrusions, or the way he had landed again and again upon her soft, yielding flesh. She must try to forget how he clutched her breasts in his hands. Or how, remarkable for a woman of her size, she had managed to lock her legs around him, tucking her dainty heels into the small of his back. Already she can barely recall the sweetness of his lips as they pressed against hers. *Imagine, his kissing her throughout their lovemaking!* Although she had no orgasm herself, she feels satisfied, and exhausted.

She realizes then that sometimes the memories of sex are even hotter than the actual event. And that, fortunately, all memories fade.

August 2

Just before dawn. Cradled in the treetops is a full and luscious moon, the rich white of cream. It reminds me of the image of the soul I was given as a Catholic schoolgirl. I was told that the soul was white and circular, solid yet translucent. It lived somewhere within my body below my head but above my navel.

I remember Sister Yvonne drawing the circle on the blackboard and using the side of the chalk to fill it in. I remember that sound, the tedious screeching that purified and made white our spiritual innards. Once she completed the soul's immaculate state, she took a felt eraser and repeatedly smacked a corner of it against the soul. Even at seven years of age, I knew repressed anger when I saw it. We were all lifted a couple inches from our seats every time the eraser marred the soul. Once when she uglied the poor thing with many blows, Sister Yvonne explained that as bad as that was, these were only venial sins. These misdemeanors offended God, but they weren't enough to anger Him sufficiently to condemn our second-grade souls to the fires of eternal hell.

Now for us, the time between Ash Wednesday and our next piece of chocolate at Easter was an eternity. It was hard to grasp that length of time over and over again without end, spent in a place that was always on fire. We were curious about the level of sin that would send you there. That's when we were told about mortal sin. That sin is committed when you did something really wrong, and you knew it was a serious offense, and you did it anyway. She took her eraser and removed all the white chalk from the soul, leaving it a creamy, dreary black.

The empty circle was doomed.

But luckily, she said, there was hope. It was then that we learned about the horrors of the confessional. You had to tell a priest all about your mortal sins and their frequency in exact numbers. You then were instructed by the priest (who represented God) to say the same prayers over and over in order to be forgiven. This information busied our little minds with many bothersome questions. I never saw my parents step into a confessional...were they doomed? What if I committed a sin that I thought was venial but was really mortal...did God make allowances for that miscalculation? We lied to our parents all the time...what if we miscounted and confessed the wrong number of times? Would that one omission be our one-way ticket to eternal damnation? Some nights I barely slept.

Our lives continue to be complex and messy things as adults. Our questions on morality are obfuscated by more questions on intent, frequency, or defining the gray areas. What are the mortal sins of today? Same as 3,000 years ago? If you refer to the Ten Commandments delivered to Moses on Mount Sinai, we're all in a little trouble. We don't honor those we should and we steal, lust, and covet. We worship false idols, usually high-end commercial goods, and forget about keeping holy the Sabbath. That's the perfect day, after a quick mass, to head out to Home Depot or cut the grass because we work so obsessively all week it's the only chance we have. "On that day," it is instructed in the Book of Exodus (which has nothing to do with driving in droves back to Manhattan on Sunday night), "no one is to work—neither you, your children, your slaves, your animals, nor the foreigners who live in your country." So take the yoke off your dog and give the Guatemalans the day off.

We don't like to be too hard on ourselves. We know our motives are usually just and defensible. And should we transgress, we are most anxious to forgive ourselves. You have to be able to sleep at night.

I am guilty of much of this. My behavior and emotions have felt out of my control, but is that really true? Have I simply made easy but bad choices? Who have I harmed? Have I sinned? If I have, who will rank my sins for me and determine my penance? Who is to blame and who is to be forgiven? God only knows.

The screaming can be heard throughout the trailer park. It penetrates every window, opened or closed.

"Fuck you, Rae! And your fucking faggot boyfriend!" Sonny's words fly from the kitchen window into the night's dense cloud of mosquitoes. "Who's next? Who is fucking *left?*"

"Get off it, will you, Sonny," Rae shoots back. "This jealousy thing is getting really stale. There was no commitment ceremony held in the back seat of your pick-up. This whole family thing was your idea, not mine!"

"Shut up, Rae. Six'll hear you."

"It's got nothing to do with Six. It's about you thinking that this little arrangement we have means *you* control what *I* do. You can have your heirloom tomatoes and your Budweiser and your whole goddam dream. But I pay the bills, Sonny. I diddle with anybody I like. That clear? So fuck you back. You don't own me."

She turns her back and starts washing dishes, which she never does.

"Rae." She doesn't turn around.

"What is it now, Sonny?"

It's the *now* that hurts him most. She wants to know if there is one more trivial thing he must bring up at this point. He hates how she makes his anger so insignificant. He wants to hit her, hard, again and again. His right arm is even twitching. But he knows he never has and he can't now. So he releases his rage with a sobbing, muffled at first and then with a pathetic heaving. He lowers his heavy, bobbing head and then she does turn and look at him. The way his arms hang at his sides and his back rounds in defeat, these things thin the congestion in Rae's heart a bit.

She sits him down and pulls his head into her bosom. She strokes his hair and forgives him for his inadequacies, his failed dreams, his inability to tame his shrew.

"I'm sorry this hurts you." It is a meaningless, shallow apology but it seems to calm him.

All in all, she thinks, this little affair has gone pretty well.

August 4

An old picnic table, still sturdy, just over the bluff. May have been on private property. The surface of the table was deeply rutted, but she climbed up on it anyway and lay on her back. She pulled down her shorts. No underwear. Paul was a good distance away, resting I suppose, his back to us.

She draped her long legs over the edge of the table and stared at the overcast sky above us. I read her very clearly. Get me a ticket out of town.

I was getting good at this, my new role as sexual mechanic.

I removed my shirt, all stripes and fake confidence. Rolled it up and placed it beneath her head. I put my folded jeans in the curve of her spine and under her buttocks. I tore into her, and there where so many families had passed potato salad and beans, we splintered our bodies with that sacred, familial wood. Then prayerlike on my knees for a length of time that made everything below my knees numb, I gave her the ticket she requested and sent her reeling back at least a couple of lifetimes. Once she'd caught her breath, I pulled her into a sitting position and held her tight against me. She let me do this, not out of any tenderness, only exhaustion.

Paul was nowhere to be seen.

CAN'T SEE THE WATER FOR THE WAVES

The two men stand at the water's edge, with hands shoved into pockets. One might think they are planning a transoceanic crossing by the way their squinting eyes skim the sea's expanse.

"I don't get it, man," Sonny says, his eyes still on the water. He has just seen Claude and Sloan, naked, together, and the picnic table without a picnic. "It just ain't natural. That's your wife, man." A few seconds pass, and then he looks at Paul. "Your wife!"

Paul had seen him come over the bluff; the women had not. Paul had been far enough away that they didn't notice his leaving. Sonny's eyes had never left the two women as Paul maneuvered him back down the loose sand toward the water.

"It's all right, man," Paul says.

"I don't get it. Your wife is some kind of dyke, and you say it's all right." Sonny takes hold of Paul's arm. "You just watch them?"

"You don't understand," Paul says. This is all so tiring for him.

"So you're gonna jump in there, right? I mean that's what it's all about, right? It's all for you. Because otherwise I don't get it."

Paul can feel the movement of the waves deep in his gut. His head is beginning to feel like a buoy, bobbing further and further away from his neck. He needs a bathroom.

"Of course I'm going to jump in there," he manages. "Hey, Sloan and I have been married quite awhile…things can get stale, if you know what I mean."

Sonny smiles. At last, there is something in this ass-backwards situation he can understand. "It's like a threesome then?"

"Right. I watch for awhile…get really turned on, and then…"

"Yeah, I'll give you that. It's pretty hot, seeing them together, you know, Claude on your wife like that. I didn't think she had it in her." He shakes his head and laughs.

"Well, I think I better get back there, don't you?" Paul hopes he can manage to walk in a manly, self-assured way back up the bluff.

"I'm gone," Sonny says. He almost runs away, taking off along the shoreline. "Make like I was never here," he yells without looking back.

Paul lowers himself to the sand. He has never indulged thoughts about his wife's infidelity. It's not like they had actually planned the whole thing. He really couldn't remember now whose idea it had been or what the outcome was supposed to be. It had seemed more a game than anything else. They had seen her hungover, a mess, after having slept on the beach. You could smell the stale beer on her, as if she'd been belching in her stupor. But there was something in her awkward, apologetic half-smile that had gotten to them both. It also could have been the way her boyish haircut contrasted with the heavy curve of her breasts beneath her half-open shirt. Or just simply how pathetic and completely lost she looked. Maybe he was naive, but to him, it had really just happened, this tryst between his wife and this woman. It had simply unraveled like everything else had this final summer.

There was that first time, he remembers, when his wife had gone to her, had sat behind her, touched her, had scared the poor thing away. Hadn't she done that for him, to please him in some way? They hadn't made love in months. He was still very affectionate, but had no appetite or interest in having sex with her. There's another thing, he realizes, that cancer steals from you...your passion.

There had been none of that slithering away and lying associated with a common affair. He was always there with them, *wasn't he?* A spark of doubt flares in his mind. There is no need to think about it, he tells himself. This affair with Claude has been only a distraction, just something to relieve the choking poignancy of each day's passing.

And he knows for certain that sex works for Sloan. It keeps her in this world and helps release some of the emotional muck of her past. More than love, sex will help keep her sane.

Just now, he hadn't been able to take his eyes off Claude. Her body movements, the way she read his wife, how her hands had traveled over Sloan's body. *Was he envious? Grateful?* No, not either of those things...some mix of the two and a thousand others.

But something had changed. For him? For her? Paul then realizes that change has been the gamble in this whole game.

Then he feels Sloan's presence. She spreads her legs and sits directly behind him. He hates the nauseating way she smells at that moment. She whispers his name in his ear.

He pulls her hands into his chest as he watches Claude walk west down the beach. Her head is lowered but he perceives a lightness in her gait.

Perhaps, Paul concludes, he has underestimated them both.

PENTOBARBITAL AND MERLOT

At the dead end of summer, in the unbearable, unbreathable company of August, Paul confirms to Claude what she already knows, that he is dying. He has cancer of the pancreas. No treatment will save him so he has chosen none. Hasn't she noticed his weight loss? His fatigue and lack of appetite? Or the pain that is so clearly etched in the contours of his face? Claude nods slowly, but doesn't know what to say.

They sit with their backs against the booth wall and face together the water and all his physiological details. He describes how bilirubin is manufactured in the liver and travels down the bile duct, how it passes through the pancreas just before emptying into the duodenum, which leads into the small intestine.

Paul stops here and they listen to the joyful, shrieking voices of children in the shore-breakers. The water is rough and noisy and throwing the little bodies over and over back to shore.

"The tumor is blocking the bile duct. Bilirubin is building up in my blood. Haven't you noticed the jaundice in my eyes?" She has been distracted, has indeed not noticed, but doesn't say this.

Then he tells her more about his wife. How her brother had died when she was very young and so in love with him. In brief but tortuous detail, he tells of the boy's drowning right in front of her. A veil fell over her eyes, her entire life, he says, from this unbearable pain suffered at such a delicate age.

Claude delivers her only question. "Why does all this involve me?" She regrets immediately the callous, selfish sound of those words.

"I am afraid that she will disappear completely into herself. Feeling anything at all for you might discourage that."

Claude is bothered by the "at all" and barely hears what follows. Sloan had been drawn to her, he mumbles on. She can't fathom her saying that. She can't imagine a word of the conversation between them when this idea of theirs evolved. She listens again to the screaming of the children and the breaking surf. A car radio belches out a bass line as it pulls into the lot. She watches Paul and sees his lips moving, but she hears nothing. When she does tune in again, he is describing his plan for his last day—dawn on the first Friday of September, the beach, his wife, the pentobarbital, their favorite local Merlot. And her.

"I want nothing to do with this. I'm not your witness or her insurance policy on sanity." Claude says these words slowly, angrily, but they mix syllable by syllable into the cacophony surrounding them. Paul now has his head in his hands and she can't tell what impact her words had on him. She's not sure if he heard them at all.

August 6

I have known him over this short time to be frail and delicate. Had I noticed the yellowing of his eyes? No. That he was in pain, not well? Yes. I have been a narcissistic child. I have seen and felt acutely, but selectively.

I do care for him. But nothing much came to me during his revelation. Not sadness, not surprise, only anger.

What does she need to exist in the world without him? I suppose any release for the pain, for the loss, from the past will do.

I will do.

"I *am* sorry, Paul."

Paul doesn't look at Claude. He is watching the last bit of sun dance on the grasses outside. He has nearly forgotten their conversation from the day before.

"In my dreams, I have no pain, no limitations of any kind," he says. "Boundless energy and a perfect body. I never question what I can or can't do. But after sleeping, my life is the nightmare I wake up to. And then the next night, I slowly leave my pathetic body as I drift off. Again in the morning my dying is a cold slap in the face. And then I pretend to be engaged in the things I pretend to care about."

He looks at Claude. His kitchen is drifting into darkness. "Cancer is not a growth. It's a deficit. It's the increasing emptiness where your life used to be."

"I don't know what to say."

"It's easy. Just say you'll be there. I'll do the dying. I'm not a coward. I'm not afraid of death."

After a long silence he continues. "They've all assured me I'll lose this battle, so I choose to sign a treaty with death before the really serious fighting begins. I'm a vain man. I don't want Sloan to see my body in ruins and my mind clouded by pain medications. I don't want her to nurse me, to shovel tasteless food in my mouth, or watch me transform into a useless, hideous shell of a man. That will not be her last impression of me."

He walks to the windows that face the water. "I'm not asking you to condone any of this, Claude. It's already decided. I did not choose death. It chose me. *It chose me!* In September, I'll only be accepting that fate. Be there for Sloan. Just be there for her."

Paul turns, takes her hand, and leads her to the door. "Please go. I've had this same conversation so many times with myself. I'm sick of it."

August 8

What connection does he fantasize I have with her?

Does he think I'll still want her once he's gone? Will there be anything left of her to desire?

August 11

Later than usual, almost 11:00. Thought we'd had the last of this insanity.
He's too sick. She's too desperate. I'm too angry.

It is clear that Paul is disappearing. In contrast, Sloan seems to grow in a
brooding density. As they neared my booth she dragged her long toes through
the sand and hung her head. So slow was their progress toward me I won-
dered if they were moving at all. Her arm came around his waist. His face
was raised to the sun in defiance. Once they finally were close, she gave me
that concentrated look, on me and just past me all at once. If this had been a
movie, I would have walked out.

Not a word was spoken, but Paul eased a smile in my direction of such
warmth, it made me shiver. Maybe his anger and impatience had eased.

Out came my loyal metal money box to perform my official duties and we
were off to the pines. It was so hot and humid the scent from the trees there
was nauseatingly sweet. Paul sat down with his back against a pine trunk.
Closed his eyes. His wife came immediately to me and I dutifully
undressed her.

When I looked over at him over her bare shoulder, his eyes were on us. Those
delicate eyelids, a skim of skin half-lowered, could have been read as seduc-
tive. His entire body looked loosely strung together, in the shade as brown as
the tree he was propped up against. I felt something new for him. It wasn't
pity or even compassion. Just a broad, intense connection, like between two
airline passengers facing a desperate landing together.

Her body pumped mechanically against me as I went inside her. I did man-
age to see him smiling at her, his dear Sloan, on the day of her graduation
from consciousness. Their eyes locked.

Then we both witnessed her loud and noxious orgasm.

We didn't eat; I don't remember now if they even brought anything. But we
slept, each close by but in a private lair. We were a tight little universe of
three spinning, exhausted planets. The heavy August air held us close to the
earth for an hour or so. I came to before they did and occupied myself with

the pine needle indentations on my knees. Watched them sleeping there, now touching fingertips. I was responsible for holding the planets in orbit, which was challenging because I felt so lightheaded and anxious. I didn't belong there, but I couldn't leave them.

She hovers protectively over her battered notebook, penciling long lines across the pages. The evening's air is thick, oppressive and lodges itself into the wavy cardboard cover of the book. The pages have lost their original crispness and are now more like cloth than paper. Claude sits on a rise of dune only a short distance from where she had been with Paul and Sloan many hours before. Now she is free of the trees and facing the water.

The lovely blue stain of twilight saturates the sky. Still, there's enough light to write and she is oblivious to the beauty of the sun's setting. To her, it's simply getting dark and a degree or two cooler.

Then Claude does hear the music and she realizes it's been there for some time. Aretha Franklin, beyond a doubt, pumping life and jubilation into a melody. She raises her head and sees that Aretha is blasting from a tape player in the sand down the beach. "If I lose this dream I don't know what I'm gonna do…"

Claude backs closer to the rim of trees, but she can still hear the happy spurts of brass and the guitar and piano. Then Aretha exhales a note so pure and perfect, Claude feels it bounce against the backside of her soul. She closes her eyes. "Help me hold on to this dream for sometimes dreams often come true."

She opens her eyes and now Claude sees the four dancers down there on the beach, tearing up the sand and the last orange lick of sunset. There is Paul and Rae with Six and Cherry. They look to Claude so wispy, fine as spirits, like Matisse's dancers. In a circle they move, together and alone, forever ancient and brimming with youth, each one to the other a smile, a laugh, singing along with the goddess of this ritual, the crowned queen of soul.

Claude sits back on the bluff. She watches as Rae's undulations drill her down into the sand in a dance as old as procreation itself. Rae's breasts are wrapped in only the suggestion of a bathing suit, making them free and joyous orbs. She sees Paul moving slowly as if swept by a gentle wind. His limbs fly freely around him, and with eyes closed he feels his way through the music and the twilight. On his lips, a smile, perhaps of gratitude for the energy, the company, the fine music.

Six is a nymph with small, pointed ears and dirty feet that look like black socks from where Claude sits. She skips and spins and shakes her hands as she circles around the purple, plastic music player.

And then there's Cherry. Elegant in a flowing gauze skirt, she melds unabashedly disco moves with some Martha Graham. She twists and lunges with arms wide open, then twirls with one arm raised in playful artistry. She takes Six in her arms and spins, then does the same with Paul, but more slowly.

And Aretha prays on, "...if it goes away, I might as well hang it up, 'cause I don't know if I have the heart or mind to make it true, or help it grow."

Claude understands something very clearly as she watches them move to the music in the fading light. Of these four dancers on the beach, not one cares right now about September, school, or unfaithful lovers. They are all mindlessly lost in the glorious, perfect music and the last bit of the disappearing sun on the tail end of summer. It is one dance they dance, ancient and wild. It is as pure of purpose as pointless folly and as essential to life as breath. Through the shared music and movement, Claude watches the boundaries of skin and predicament dissolve. Rae transmutes into a black poet dying of pancreatic cancer, and Six is now a transvestite prone to fits of jealousy and imperfect forgiveness. Cherry metamorphoses into a truant child of great spiritual depth, and Paul becomes a woman not only capable of sexual overindulgence but also of great compassion. They are drunk and giddy and free, and Claude envies them greatly.

The song ends. Cherry folds in half at the waist and hits the off button on the tape player. There is more laughter and bits of lyrics as they weave together, arm in arm, and walk away from Claude into what is now almost night.

"Baby, baby, hold on," Rae sings with a sexy, absentminded loveliness. And too soon for Claude, they and the singing are gone.

August 12

I saw her today. She was walking on the Main Road, hands in her pockets, beautiful long legs slicing through space. I was at the Blue Light and she was heading towards the causeway. Her dangling head was hidden by a hat, uncommon for her, just a straw farmer's hat with a ragged brim. As she passed the restaurant, she was so close I could see the wet blotches on the front of her white undershirt, the kind old men and teenagers wear. Was the wetness from perspiration? Tears? A public water fountain? A few steps more and she pulled off that hat and threw it by the roadside. Kept walking on with her head down, but at a faster clip, away from me.

Rose appeared with a tall glass of cool white wine and a plate of fresh oysters, neither of which are on the menu. I drank the wine in three long slugs. I hate oysters. She was half right.

My meal was three dollars, an indication that many out here know the sad shape I'm in. I walked along the road, picked up Sloan's hat, and headed for the salt marsh. The earth was on fire and the day stretched aimlessly before me. Too much had happened too early.

I craved relief. Thought of emptying this pain into my camera. Seemed too much work.

It seems pathetic now, but I dropped into the broken grasses, pulled my jeans and underwear to my knees, and thought of nothing and no one, only of a mindless release. I would have done anything, any drug, to be somewhere else.

Back at my booth, I brought in the few dollars from the fee box, raked up the cigarette butts around the picnic tables, and made an overly detailed drawing of an arbor I would build near the bathhouse, complete with the list of materials.

Then I took my camera and gear east along the shore and I captured a series of tumultuous exposures that stripped any remaining sexual energy. Again and again, I cocked and released the shutter and forced the elements into frantic compositions. I was free of thought, free of emotion, free of past and future. I'd found a better drug. Working from somewhere outside my body,

I became the sea water, the molecules that massed so willingly as stone, and the abrasive force of millions of seeds of sand. I captured the pulse of the sea as it beat upon the shore. I worked as a verb, direct and unadorned. Search. Witness. Focus. Release. Construct. Cock. Release. I took the film from my camera when I'd finished and threw it into the trash bin. I got what I needed.

But all to no good purpose. Tonight, with the straw hat held against me, the longing emerges from the swamp, ugly and demanding. My obsession has metastasized. Getting so little has me wanting so much more. But more what? To possess her? To protect her? To dissolve the pain she'll suffer with his dying?

There is one small problem. She has no true desire, no love for me. I'm merely her current drug, her heroin, her booze. His dying won't bring her to me. If that's even what I want.

Sloan runs to the park. It is early in the morning, just before seven. She explodes into Claude's booth and finds her sleeping on the floor on a pillow and a pile of photographs and papers, wearing only her underpants and a t-shirt.

"What's wrong?" Claude says. She stares at the woman standing above her. Sloan looks possessed and she's soaking wet. Claude wonders if perhaps she has willed Sloan there, that the intensity of her pathetic longing has reconstructed her in this booth cell by cell.

"Is Paul all right?"

Sloan says nothing but collapses to the floor and then sits with her thighs drawn up tight against her chest. Claude rises and facing her asks, "Is Paul okay? Does he need me? Open your mouth, Sloan."

"I had this dream," she says, eyes bulging. "There is a horse in this big tent, like a circus tent, you know, with all the colors on top." She stops and her eyes go a little crossed-eyed as her gaze falls to her nose.

"Go on," Claude says, gradually waking up to the fact that Sloan is there alone, sitting so childlike, actually speaking in full sentences. There is a sharp pain in her neck from sleeping flat on the floor. "The circus tent?"

"The top is very thin, and the sun is spinning the colors on the dirt floor inside the tent. It's really kind of beautiful." She speaks slowly, almost mumbling. Her eyes seem to follow the images in her head as she continues.

"The horse is dusty...dusty black. He's got a long, tangled mane of light gray and dark gray."

She is quiet for a few more minutes, but is shivering. Claude picks up a blanket and drapes it around her.

Sloan then tells her that she feels drawn to the horse, but is afraid of it, of its power and unpredictability. She sees the horse running, galloping hard, and circling the perimeter of the tent, bringing clouds of dust rising from the ground.

Sloan then describes how she feels the pounding vibration of the horse's huge hooves in the soles of her feet, and how, somehow, she is no longer just watching the horse gallop, but is riding bareback on him, her hands disappearing into his matted mane. Her legs are wrapped around the barrel of his midsection, her head low as the horse pounds on faster and faster. She can feel the animal's power, all manic and explosive. And then the circle they trace becomes smaller and tighter; the dirt rising so densely that she can't see much more than a blur of color, only feels the force of their rapid spinning around and around in smaller and smaller circles.

"The walls of the tent are coming in closer. I feel sick, my stomach in my throat. The horse can't handle the angle of the turns and the speed. His legs slide away from beneath him, toward the middle of the tent. I think we'll both be hurt bad but his legs don't hit the ground and we are caught in midair and keep falling and falling."

That is when, Sloan says, she woke up. She was dizzy and almost reached the toilet before she threw up.

And then, as abruptly as she had entered, she leaves the booth, still wrapped in Claude's blanket.

August 14

She brought back my blanket and another dream early this morning. I am now also her dream exorcist.

She began the retelling of the dream by describing the simple excitement of riding, feeling the power of the horse's body beneath her, the pure pleasure of the rushing air. And then she spoke briefly of her past. She talked about riding a horse in Michigan along a lake's edge.

This now becomes the most intimate thing we've shared. Actual words.

In this dream they were traveling on, she didn't know where, but not in the tent. They were moving on a flat landscape in a straight path. No trees, no sea or sky, only color speeding by, all images blurred by their great speed. Blues with streaks of yellows and reds. She described a mindless, perfect happiness as she rode her dream horse.

She has been wordless for so long. I was keyed to her every syllable. I tried to determine if her voice suited the rest of her. It was deep for a woman, and I could still hear the Michigan in it, the way she pulled on certain words and then bit off others abruptly.

Then she was silent. Something had changed for her. Cloud cover muted the low sun outside and my booth darkened melodramatically. Sloan sat motionlessly for some time. Only her eyes told me things were happening in her dream that she wasn't telling me. I didn't coax. I waited.

After a few minutes, she went on. She said that everything had changed. She was still riding fast, but she slid somehow from the horse's back to underneath it, and she realized that she was naked. I told her not to worry, that always happens in dreams, but she continued on as if I hadn't said a word.

She was still clutching the dense mane on either side, but hanging beneath the horse with her heels dug into its rib cage. The smell of the animal engulfed her. She saw blood spreading down her ankles and streaking around her legs in the wind. Was it her blood or the horse's? She didn't know.

She was afraid she'd lose her grip and fall beneath the animal. So she pulled her body tighter to him and locked her ankles and fingers above him.

Of course, this is not possible. It's a dream.

She went on and on about feeling his fluid muscles against her own naked body, the thin layer of sweat between them. How she loved the speed and danger and that she was no longer afraid of his power.

I saw where this was going.

Finally, she said, she was awake, in her bed with Paul. She was hot and panting like an animal. She didn't feel human. She was very turned on. She had to masturbate to relieve the pressure and the heat and the memory.

She admitted almost apologetically that she slid her hand down her belly and found that her underpants were already halfway to her knees. She masturbated. She came quickly and even though it was intense, Paul never woke up. Or pretended not to.

She did look at me then and gave me a very meek little grin. I leaned closer to her, but she was already getting up from the floor and we had an awkward minor collision. And then she scampered off. But in that moment near her body I did feel the heat coming from her and inhaled that scent of wet sand she carried from her sleep. I'm ashamed to admit how aroused I was, from the dream and from the too real image of her masturbating, with Paul there, probably awake. Maybe he's grown accustomed to being a wordless and somewhat disinterested witness to his wife's raw sexuality unleashed.

Why didn't she share her dream with him? It is so very much about him.

Of course, that's why.

She is never bothered by the child. She has in her own mind adopted the wild, unruly misfit as her own. She relishes seeing her rip through their bed of impatiens, shortcutting to the beach. She knows that Six is fond of her as well. Mrs. Saugerties can tell by the child's easy smile toward her and how Six will sometimes leave a lovely shell or beach stone on the plate where cookies had been left out for her. The woman envies the child's confidence—even insolence—when dealing with her husband. He, of course, finds Six dirty and undisciplined, and predicts she will evolve into some wild creature living in the woods and mating with wolves. "Better to mate with wolves than my one-minute man," Mrs. Saugerties says to the breakfast dishes waiting for her in the sink.

She runs water over them, but only a trickle so as not to waste. He hates waste. She starts the washing up. She prides herself on keeping their little home tidy, but long ago tired of cooking his favorite meals, over and over. And the laundry, she thinks of how it all must be washed by hand and hung to dry outside. Her husband prefers this method to using the miniature washer and dryer in their mobile home because they just waste electricity and rip the clothes to shreds. She knows that this is pure silliness, but she does have the time to do it all by hand. What else would she do, she wonders, go for lunch at the Blue Light? That would never happen, also being a wasteful use of money. But the thought of the eternal scrubbing and ringing out of his graying Jockey briefs with the flabby elastic waistband feeling like overcooked noodles in her hands…well, she tries not to think about that either as she finishes the dishes. Best not to dwell on how she labors from early morning until well after their supper over tedious, repetitive, and she realizes, often unnecessary tasks.

So, naturally, it is refreshing to see the child, or to feel her really. Six feels like a force of nature howling through her staid and painfully predictable world.

She folds the dish towel in half and neatly drapes it over its bar. She knows it will never dry on this hot, humid morning. Mrs. Saugerties can't remember how many days it has threatened to but never has rained. She feels off, a little dizzy, and very tired suddenly, so she lies down to rest.

Outside, her husband is tightening bolts and generally fussing with his satellite dish. When he stoops to pick up a wrench, Six comes charging through his yard, her head twisted, eyeing her homemade flag as it sails behind her. She wants Mrs. Saugerties to see her creation, but in her excitement and distraction, slams into her husband's lowered head. The collision knocks him back into a sitting position and sends the girl careening into the supports of the satellite dish. This leaves a gash on the bridge of her nose and a messy scrape across her left cheek.

She stares at Saugerties as she wipes the dirty back of her hand through the blood on her face in a cowboy, down-but-not-out maneuver. She calculates if she has time to get up and away before he stands up and smacks her.

But he sits frozen there, glaring. "You rotten little delinquent! Look at what you've done running pell mell into my yard! Why aren't you in school?"

"It's August, you old fool," Six says.

"Get the hell off my property before I give you the whipping of your life!" And as he gets to his feet and raises his hand—just to threaten her, only to scare her off—his wife sees something else entirely when she opens the aluminum screen door. Both man and child turn toward the squawking hinges and see her standing there looking back and forth between the two. She sees the blood on the girl's face. She's heard the threat delivered by her husband.

"Don't you dare..."she stammers as she comes fully out on the deck, "harm this child." There are tears on her cheeks and then her face flames with heat, and she clutches her chest and falls forward down the three narrow steps into a contorted position on the ground. The last three words she hears are someone else's name.

It is Six screaming as she springs up and runs away, "Rae! Rae! Rae!"

Rae arrives a few minutes later, barely dressed and wearing the anxious look that results from an emergency awakening. She finds Saugerties standing motionless a few feet away from his wife, staring at her as though she is a crumpled foreign object just fallen from space.

Sloan and the horse are falling through air. She sees that there is nothing above them but a blank, colorless sky. With great effort, she pulls her head down against the rushing wind of their descent and sees far below a body of water, like a pond. Is it deep enough to accommodate their speed and weight? She can't determine. Rain is falling beneath them, oddly, as if she and the horse were clouds sending millions of drops of rain to the pond.

The sensation of their joined mass racing downward terrifies her. Sloan is unable to swallow the air that sticks in her throat. She's blinded by the tears in her eyes, and everywhere pressing against her is the concrete blast of air that throbs with the constant thudding of hooves. She holds tight to the mane, the insides of her legs again strapped around the barrel of the horse. Her eyes try to find the water below them, but it appears to be falling farther away.

Her last thought before waking is that land and sky have reversed, and that she will forever be falling into a blank, bottomless expanse.

Again she wakes drenched in sweat; her mouth so dry she can barely swallow. She gets out of bed and spends the next hour or so emptying Paul's dresser drawers, refolding his clothes, putting them back in. In the top drawer she finds the box of poems and she neatens the scraps of paper inside, but does not read even one of them.

A COMMON WHITE STONE

SHE LOVES LIZARDS & FROGS
SHE THINKS I KNEW QUEEN ELIZABETH
SHE THINKS I KNOW EVERYTHING
SHE'S SURPRISED TO FIND THAT I DON'T

Mark Giles, "Spring Blossom"

Six's toes are buried in the sand. Her fingers stretch from her small hand and tug at the ragged hem of Paul's shorts. They can both feel the somber weight of the gray veil of sky pressing down on them.

"'He who believes in me, from within him there shall flow rivers of living water,'" she recites. "Do you believe that?"

"Oh, I do believe in the rivers of living water," Paul says. "These waters are filled with life, and with lost souls. I think that's why the sun sparkles on the water's surface. All those souls. Think of it."

She lets go of him and stands. Above him now with small hands nestled on hips, she is impatient with his poetic dodging. "I mean, do you believe in *God?*"

"I believe in the sun and the power of the wind. I believe past lives are still with us, you know, the people we've loved and lost. You can hear their voices late at night. Just go to the water's edge. You'll hear a breathy low wail, like the buzz in the still air after a monk stops his chanting. The sound is soothing as it travels over the expanse of the ocean and settles into your ears. The song of life, Six, and death. The song is one and the same."

"What are you talking about? You don't believe in God. You're afraid to say it." She pauses a full minute. Her brows are squeezed together with such effort that a small pellet of sweat runs down the side of her face. She feels an urge to run, to get away from him. He seems different to her all of a sudden. Her stomach is a tight fist and she hates the hot, heavy feeling in her head. "You…you are gonna die. Rae told me you probably got AIDS. And Sonny thought so, too. He thinks you're not right. But for sure I know you're sick. That's right, ain't it, Paul?"

There is a long silence before Paul's response.

"You're nine years old now, Six, and I'm going to respect that fact by telling you the truth. Dying is a subject that many adults lie about, as though it could never happen. I think that makes them feel better. But you are a courageous girl…" Here he smiles and pulls her eyes to his, "and I wouldn't dare lie to you. Yes, I am going to die, and it will be sooner rather than later. I do have some choices left."

"Well, you know, maybe you'll get better," she argues. "I can take care of you. I can cook for you and you won't be so skinny and tired. Tired is what's making you want to give up."

He sets his eyes on the harbor. "Honey, it's not the kind of sick where you get better. I have a lot of pain. I'm sure you sense this. My energy is being sapped by this sickness—fighting this cancer will take more and more out of me, until that's all my body will be doing, fighting this. And losing."

Six feels her anger trying to get out of her. She is ashamed of him and his giving up. He wants to die, so let him go ahead and die, she thinks. Her cheeks take on the color and hardness of an old, copper pan. With a steady voice she asks, "And losing means you die?" Not really a question.

"I will die before I've lost everything and I'm useless. I won't let that happen." His eyes focus on a dingy that seems to have come loose and is just bobbing free in the middle of the water.

Paul reaches down and picks up a common white stone. He holds it out for her to examine. "If I throw this stone way out in the water, can you find it? No. But is it gone? No. If you think hard enough about it, you can see it there, safe on the bottom. If you dive for it, you'll probably never recover it, but you might find something even more valuable. And the stone, my stone, is the reason you're looking in the first place."

He knows that he has lost her but continues on. "We are both in the water together, the living water as you called it."

She stands and takes the stone from his open palm. She throws it as hard as she can far into the bay. She then aims her eyes—hard, dark little assault weapons—on him. "Stones aren't alive, they're dead. And you'll be dead and it'll be your fault. The God you don't believe in won't care. You won't be in the water. You'll be in hell!"

Paul wants to respond, but before he can, she adds, "And I won't miss you one bit." And with this she runs from him, not stopping until her bare feet begin to ache and actually bleed.

August 18

She found me setting the cedar posts for the bathhouse arbor. I kept working while she stood there and delivered more pieces from her recurring dream puzzle. Was she stripteasing away layers of her subconscious for me?

She was riding her horse again and the ground beneath them was a smooth, luxurious mud, flying in slow motion in all directions, coating the under-belly of the horse as they galloped along. She heard the muscular pounding of the hooves. The pounding became a chant, mimicking her heartbeats. She said she could hear the slushing movement of her blood as clearly as the hooves. The combined sounds were deafening.

I added more post mix to the hole, then water. She went on. Seemed not to need my full attention.

She and the horse were rushing toward a bluff. They were moving so fast she was afraid they wouldn't be able to stop. Then she saw the horse's legs tumble over the cliff's edge and fall and fall. She was both on the animal and watching from a distance. They landed in deep sand. But the horse's limbs were tangled, his neck twisted. His dark mane was flecked with sand and drops of blood.

Then she looked away from her dream and at me. I put down my water bucket. She squeezed her eyes closed and began shaking her head from side to side. She said she just wanted the dreams to stop. She said she hated that fucking horse.

I was a little lost in her images and the task at hand. I couldn't think of much to say, really anything that might ease her suffering. This is the bril-liant thing I came up with ... that the only person in the world she trusted was dying, was leaving her, and that I knew she was frightened and felt abandoned. Again.

She screwed up her face. She couldn't stomach what I'd said. She didn't argue with me. She simply walked away. I suppose she heard my words. They were so simple and obvious and couldn't touch her pain. I wish I could have said it better. Or said nothing.

Now I sit with her absence in my small, cold cell. Her absence seems more tangible and real than her presence was. I can almost touch the watery empty space she inhabited that followed me here. Will his absence feel the same way to her?

Her words and images come back to me, randomly, like sloshing water from my bucket. The dream replays in my mind in black and white, the rider holding on for dear life, the horse tearing up soil and sand. The horse is a pure black, but rich with detail. In a print that delicate black is difficult to render, so subtle in its tonal variations. I suppose that's why black is the color of mourning. It is a very complex, very emotional color.

I don't completely comprehend the meaning of these dreams, but her telling them to me is significant on its own. Now they've become part of my reality.

August 19

No moon, no stars, not even headlights tonight. The blackness is comforting, the way it surrounds me as intimately as my past. I would love to evaporate into the night. I want to break down. Become less. Wrap her in my darkness, whisper that it's all right, all of it.

A SPIRIT UNCLEAN

HAVE PITY ON ME, O LORD,
FOR I AM WEAK;
HEAL ME, O LORD,
FOR MY BONES ARE SHAKEN
AND MY SOUL IS DEEPLY TROUBLED

Psalm 6:3-4

Six walks along the Sound east of Cherry Grove on her way to Paradise. She had named this rocky lick of beach as such because of the time she had been sitting there, memorizing the Psalms she loved. The royal-blue sky had been filled with fluffy, white clouds, with sunlight falling in visible streams to earth. It had created in her mind a holy card picture of heaven, her own promise of paradise.

Today, however, the sun is hidden and her mood is dark. As she walks on, she feels her spirit is weak and she has the sense that it follows a few feet behind her, separate and unknown. Nothing feels right in her universe. Six thinks about the angry God of the Old Testament and then of the finicky Sioux spirits of nature taught to her by her father. She is certain, no matter how you look at it, that people have undying souls. Only on this does she agree with Paul. She wonders if he knows that those who sin against God's laws lose their immortal souls to the fires of hell. Then there is also the eternal scorn of your ancestors for serious wrongdoing. Every act for her, even her skipping school, is part of the big struggle between good and evil. On every decision, you will be judged.

Once she reaches Paradise, she sits on the boulder with the cupped top, where she always sits. She stares at the sky and finds no breaks in the low ceiling above, only layer upon layer of gray clouds edged in a blackish blue. She can sense quite clearly the displeasure of both God and nature weighing upon them all.

Six doesn't open her Bible, but leaves it tucked beneath her right thigh. She sits motionlessly and does not pray. If she was the type of girl who cried, she thinks, she would cry right now.

"All right you hateful, old prick, I've brought you some chicken from last night's dinner. Don't worry your shabby little head, I cooked it to death so it's as dry and bland as you are." Then she chides herself; she's being too hard on this barely conscious man. "Sorry, that's harsh. I've brought you some white bread, eggs, and milk, and some new Jockey briefs you seem to favor. I cannot bear to wash those foul things you've been wearing."

Cherry walks across his perfect lawn, steps over his deceased wife's failing impatiens, and climbs the steps of Saugerties' mobile home. She wiggles around him as he sits in his aluminum chair with the hideous green canvas straps that are, to her horror, the very same color as his faux shutters. It is the stench of him, however, that brings Cherry's hand to cover her nose and mouth as she passes.

"Oh Gaaawd! You smell like shit, which I use not as a simile but as a completely accurate appraisal. What? You don't know what a simile is? You need a lot of educating, but we'll start with this. A simile is the use of *like* or *as* to connect two similar things. You'd like another example?"

Saugerties looks up at her with a blank expression. Then he smiles.

"Okay then. You look as crazy as makeup on a corpse. Oh stop me! You're putting ideas in my head." She laughs at her own silliness and then takes a hard, sobering look at her old foe. "I will put these things away, and then I will stand you in the shower where you will undress and wash yourself. That I will never do."

This is where Cherry usually finds him, propped on his former throne on the small deck like some deposed monarch, stripped of his authority and the will to rule. He has aged noticeably in the few days since his wife died. When people in Cherry Grove speak of her passing, beyond "such a sweet woman," there are comments regarding the myocardial infarction she had suffered, and how it seemed so massive for such a petite, unassuming woman. Rae had noted and others had agreed that the poor woman had most likely imploded from all her squelched comments, all the lip-biting, all the resentment never expressed. "Say what you want about the modern woman," Rae had said, "but she was the type of girl nobody wants to be anymore."

Cherry knows that Rae's type isn't so popular either—a freewheeling, unrestrained woman who does not respect the property of others. Rae has just gone to the opposite extreme.

Cherry feels more akin to the old-fashioned, devoted sort of wife, a woman like Mrs. Saugerties, who did have a sweet if not a strong heart. And Cherry is surprised to discover in herself compassion for the other casualty, the hollow shell of a man that has sat here on his deck day into night since his wife passed. Cherry is sure it has been the force of his grief that has caused his stupor. Now he often drivels on about odd, nonsensical things, sometimes whole sentences about his neighbors or things he should do to the lawn or shrubbery. There are also mumbled, vague apologies to no one in particular. He never utters his wife's name or makes any mention of her.

It doesn't matter to Cherry whether his apologies are to her, or his wife, or the universe. It doesn't matter that this man symbolizes all the hatred the world and her own family have heaped upon her. He needs her now and she will care for him as best she can. Sometimes life is just that simple.

So when it rains, she will bring him indoors, like a pet. She will make sure that there is food in the house and that the place is reasonably clean. He is a changed man and requires little care or entertainment. He never watches his television anymore. Never flies his flag. Barely acknowledges her assistance or even her presence.

After his shower this morning, Cherry feeds him the cold chicken, piece by piece, as though he is a baby and cannot feed himself. As she does this, she freely examines his face. Anger has contorted his features into an extreme terrain, tire-rutted, and bristles poke from his jowls. But now something else is also present, a vulnerability that tugs at her.

"I'll get your Remington and clean you up," she tells him. "And tomorrow I'll come by with my clippers and impose a little style into that hairdo of yours. What is it you go for, something in the nature of Dwight Eisenhower?"

Had Saugerties any sanity or humanity left in him, he might have sought forgiveness for his bigotry toward Cherry, or for everything that had happened at No Gun Ri. He might have regretted his dismissal of the faint sound of his wife's own pleasure, alone in their bed, that he often had heard as he washed up in their tiny bathroom after sex. But those opportunities have passed, and all he has now is a lost smile for the transvestite who daily saves his life.

August 22

I've been keeping an eye on Six. She seems so changed. I'm afraid she's become some unlucky sponge, sopping up all the drama and agitation around her. There's enough tension and regret wound into this circle of sand, aluminum, and pine to send this entire trailer park swirling into the Atlantic. We have become a hubcap lost at high speed, with the poor child running after us.

Naturally, she's changed. There's heavy mud on the small feet once composed of feathers and flight. Her parents are in a firestorm, on the verge of splitting up it must feel. If only Rae would keep her affairs hidden from the child and from Sonny, but who am I to criticize? Six probably senses the intensity of my relationship with Sloan without needing to name what we do, which would be tantamount to condemning us both to hell in her mind. Children, especially this highly intuitive one, can pick up on charged sexuality as quickly as they can smell death, also horrifying but more tangible.

Which brings us to Paul, her ally, confidant, her friend. She smells death on him. I doubt he's actually told her, but if he has, I'm sure the message was so cloaked in optimism and romantic frills, his evasion would only annoy the girl. To whatever degree she knows, she knows.

Cherry has also been weirdly quiet and restrained. She watches after Saugerties, which is ironic past belief. Barton sleeps in his workshop. We all know that and we all know why. Penance. But when will it be paid in full? He eats his meals at the Blue Light and even the most intolerant locals leave him alone. In a community this small, everybody knows who's banging who, and Barton's crime might have brought him both clemency and a little respect. But not from Six.

Mrs. Saugerties has died and her husband, Six's favorite comic-book villain, now smiles blankly at Six when she crosses his yard, like she was a sweet, stray pup. I'm sure that, too, is disconcerting to her.

And, equally tragic, fourth grade looms before her, with all its frightening elements. There will be irrelevance, hard-sole shoes, idiot classmates, and life locked indoors.

I think she'd love to bring us all together, maybe in the laundry room with the rhythmic voices of the washers and dryers to calm and center us. We might become hypnotized by the sound of rushing water and the erratic clicking of metal buttons inside the dryers. Once we were quieted, the kid would instruct us to contemplate all that has happened over the course of the summer. Together we would decide how best we can salvage the messy accident that has become our lives.

But who listens to a kid?

I worry for her as though she were my own. Because that's the way it is here, just one sprawling, dysfunctional family.

August 23

I saw Paul this morning, swimming in the Sound not far from his cottage. The rising, orange sun backlit his slow efficient strokes. He disappeared beneath the water's surface, then reappeared, angled to his back and swam that way for a while. He was naked.

The sea caressed him as he moved through her mass. What would we do without this all-forgiving, loving body of water to console us, to make right all the things we have bungled or have boggled us? I could sense the simple, restorative flow of water on his flesh, maybe cooling a fever or caressing his damaged body.

The salty water held him safely near her surface. She never admonished him for his human limitations. She did not flaunt her overwhelming might. The sea could swallow him whole, could break barges in half, or chisel a new face onto the shoreline. Or she can be sweet as she is now, nursing this swimmer on a late-summer morning.

I watched from my hiding place as he walked from the water to the shore. His level head not bobbing, but like a buoy on a still sea. Then he picked up his towel and wrapped it around his waist, the long, trim waist of a boy.

Tonight I've had no dinner but drank a bottle of wine, alone. I removed my clothes and danced with the white birches. A heavy breeze provided the rhythm. I doubt anyone saw me. Who would notice one more tree, arms in the air, fingers full of darkness. The roundness of my breasts only gnarled bark. My bare feet planted in the soil plate, looking like exposed roots. No more than that.

I want to be in my body only, as he was in the sea, with the same grace and confidence. Or at least that's how he looked to me.

Once inside the cottage, Paul removes his wet towel and puts on his robe. He finds its abundance comforting but soon he grows too warm. He separates the front halves and lets his naked body breathe. How he loves this robe, a velvety blue, a gift from his wife on their first Christmas together. It was the most traditional of gifts to a husband, and he loves that, too. They had slept that night both covered by this robe in front of the fire.

Sloan is in their bedroom, lost in sleep. Even when he had kissed her neck on returning, she had not stirred. He sits now at the kitchen table and decides to write in order to understand what he is feeling. However the words come to him, so be it; that will be the finished thing. Although he is tired from his swim, the first line of the poem comes easily:

Joy is that fragile.

He puts coffee on and continues, vowing to end the poem once the coffee is ready.

The pain is real, a man with a gun.
Pain is how death robs from you the desire to live.
It swallows you up and removes your appetite.
Even when it eases, you are left weakened,
like a child after a seizure, limp and purposeless,
unable to enjoy its absence.

Oh yes, I am terrified to die,
not knowing exact timing or sequence.
Is it a morning mist that dissipates
or a sudden, violent deluge that rips a man from shore?

I'll assume the worst,
but refuse to board up windows.
Bring it on. Bring it on.
I'll puff my chest at the water's edge.
All I have to lose is life itself.

There is no mention of lost joy.

The coffee is ready. *Time to drop this sad addition into the box of poems.* He takes two mugs, long designated as hers and his. He will bring her to wakefulness with the aroma, and use his coffee only to steady his hands. He has long ago lost his taste for it.

A FINE GIFT

Six is sitting crosslegged on the ground at the entrance to the trailer park when Claude walks by. The girl is leaning with her back against the post that supports a row of aluminum mailboxes. She wears a dress, a crumpled collection of tiny yellow flowers on a blue background. It is simple, loose, and seems not overly offensive to her. There are comb tracks through her wet, wild crop of hair, and her bare feet are the dusky brown of aged leather. A pair of white sandals sit next to her.

"It's Arthur's birthday," she says without great enthusiasm. "His dad is taking us to the movies. We get our own popcorn and soda."

"What are you guys going to see?"

"I don't know, something about fish," Six says. "Arthur gets to pick."

Arthur is small for his age, and wears black-rimmed glasses of a style that suggests they had belonged to his father as a boy. He is awkward, intelligent, and shy, so he is also fair game for ridicule by his less charitable classmates.

Claude sees in her lap a wrapped parcel. There is a great deal of cellophane tape constricting a wad of colorful supermarket flyers, and a daisy is taped on top of the rectangular mess. An envelope nearby carries the words "Arther Lenerd," written in Six's distinctive scratchy style.

Claude points to the package. "What do you have there? Guess that's for the birthday boy." Six's eyes travel down to her lap. She seems surprised to see it, as if it had just fallen from the tree limb above her.

"It's my Bible."

Claude stares at the child. "How can you give that away, Six? I know it means the world to you. Did Sonny get you a new one?"

Six looks at her and says plainly, "I don't need it anymore. I memorized all the parts I like. Arthur ain't allowed to even touch his family's Bible, so he can't read it."

Claude still can't believe she is giving the book away. It is not only one of her few possessions, but also one of her most precious, right up there with her bicycle. She always holds it close to her body when she carries it, just like a little missionary. But now it lies in her lap, a lifeless thing that could be yesterday's lunch.

"Well, that's some fine gift," Claude says, and then she sits with her in silence in the dirt until Arthur's father arrives in a drained-green Ford Galaxy. Six hands the package to Arthur as soon as she climbs in, and he smiles and holds it close to his chest as they pull away.

August 24

I remember Six's recounting of a trip to mass with Arthur's family. That Sunday she came straight away to the park to tell me about the dreamy eyes of the priest as he sent smoke puffs of incense into the church. She loved the clanking sound that made; it reminded her of the bells on the buoys in the inlet. She hated the singing, but adored the heavy breathing of the organ and all the old Polish ladies in their perfect Sunday clothes. She loved it all, the way a child might love a circus come to town.

And she loved the Bible readings, delivered so slowly and with such great power. There were no better lessons. It was really all the school she ever needed, she said, unless you wanted to be a nurse or a roofer, which she did not. She was quite sure on that particular Sunday that she would like to be a priest. I didn't have the heart to tell her that her gender was banned from the priesthood, but instead I encouraged her, so seldom did she get so animated about a subject.

I do worry about her distaste for school, that it might compromise her future options. Still she seems so solid and capable, I know she'll find her way in this world.

But there by the side of the road today, I swear she was a different girl. If you observe a child carefully, you may witness rapid dramatic changes in character, in a more pronounced way than either inches or pounds or food preferences. It's as if one day she is this way, and the next day that behavior or attitude is years behind her, completely gone. One morning a child may put aside a blanket that she has never slept without, and it will become precious only to her mother. She may have been childishly afraid of the silliest things, and then one day she just stands up and dismisses them with a seriousness that reeks of adulthood.

Evidently, this battered old Bible has lost significance for Six. Something else, I have no idea what, has become more valuable to her. Perhaps her friendship with Arthur. Perhaps something else entirely.

August 25

Paul came by at midmorning, picked me up at the booth. We walked over to the picnic table that sits on the empty far end of the parking field. There's a slender view of the water there and the area feels private. We have rarely been alone together, not for any length of time.

It seems more difficult for him to walk any distance now, so I knew he was here for a reason, but he said nothing. We stared ahead at the slit of water. The silence made me uncomfortable.

The heat of the day was intensifying, rising and gathering on the water's surface, picking up humidity, rolling it directly at us through the gap in the cedars. My neck felt prickly and damp and locked into place. Paul remained motionless. I waited for him to talk but nothing came.

Maybe he simply wanted not to be alone. I moved to sit on the top of the table directly behind him, my knees at his sides, my arms gently resting on his shoulders, my hands open and flat against his chest. He relaxed into me and put his hands on mine. We sat like that for quite some time.

I felt myself being drawn into him. It was the oddest feeling. All my con- flicting emotions, all my good intentions, even my health, were moving through my hands, into his...his what? His core? His need? His despera- tion? Could I presume into his soul? I found myself connected to him in a more intense way than I have been to her. It was far more intimate. It was not a physical but a spiritual exchange and I don't pretend to know what was involved. When these things happen, it's enough to know that they have.

I cried so motionlessly and so silently that I doubt he knew. And, as is always the case when we suffer grief prematurely, I cried more for myself than for him.

A few cars came and went from the parking field during this colossal event. One couple tucked their folded bills into the fee box, but most took advantage of my absence and drove right through.

After some time, Paul turned and raised his eyes to me and, as if we'd been having a conversation all along, he said in one long, slow exhalation, "And that's all I have to tell you, my friend."

GOING ON A BENDER

It is around eight in the evening when Six joins Claude on the beach. They sit on a small bluff in the cool sand. For awhile they watch three gulls pick at the litter on the beach, their waistlines ruined by the spoils of other picnics. The sea is a deep, slate blue and the sky mottled, moody, almost violet. The gulls, by contrast, are a dazzling white.

Both Six and Claude feel the weight of the summer and that change is coming. It is not change they want. Not much feels secure or familiar. They try a little small talk about baseball, and then laugh at Cherry's fussing over Saugerties. Then follows a long stretch of silence, but it's a noisy silence that reverberates with questions not asked, fears not divulged, comfort not offered.

Finally, Claude does look at Six and finds her smiling. The girl stands and faces the water. Off comes her t-shirt as she runs in wearing only her faded camp shorts through the cooling air into the sea. She attacks the shore-breakers like only a child can do, and runs into the water with such velocity that only the increasing depth stops her. Then she throws her fierce, little frame into the vast arms of the sea with a wail of immaculate delight.

Claude, being the adult, thinks about the water temperature, the presence of jellyfish, the unknown tides. But when Six motions to her with a single flutter of fingers, she can do nothing but go with her. Claude throws off her own shirt and leaves it on the beach with all the heaviness of the past months. She goes on a bender and frees her bottled spirit first by inhaling the warm cloud of moist, salty air that hovers just above the water's surface. She takes it into her nostrils, fills her lungs, is intoxicated by it. And then the Long Island Sound pulls her forward over the small beach pebbles and into her luxuriously soft, sandy bottom.

Six rides in to meet her and together they tumble in the shore-breakers, and then laugh their way back into deeper water. They juke the night air as they repeatedly dive deep to the bottom and shoot back up. Claude feels more like a child than when she was a child. The water slides against her body, fingers her hair, rushes between her toes as she swims. It is all glorious—the weightlessness underwater, the night now upon them, the sea like a womb for twins.

Six swims between Claude's legs and then pulls them out from underneath her. As she goes down, a wave catches them both and they willingly tumble to shore and then dash out of the water. Late August nights can be unpredictable, but the coolness surprises them as they stand breathless in the moonlight and the precious stillness. Six smiles again, but now with her lips quivering and teeth chattering.

She asks Claude, does she feel better?

Claude tells her that yes, she does. Much.

She wraps her dry denim shirt around Six; it is all she has. She points her toward home. Six stumbles up the bluff, the long shirttails tripping her up, and then disappears. Claude can picture Rae scolding her as she peels off the wet clothing, toweling her hair and body. She'll ask after her missing shirt, ask if she was swimming alone. Tell her that that is something she should never do.

Claude can pretty much imagine their whole night ahead—the blue light of the baseball game on the television, the recliner holding Six and her father, the two falling asleep around the eighth inning, and then Rae leaving for the hospital. It will all feel familiar and safe for the girl. It will be August the way it used to be.

August 26

I think Six's soul is old, which is why childhood might be boring for her. She's ready for something else. I'm sure it's not a life like the adult lives around her.

What happened with Paul yesterday on the picnic bench? What was that wordless transference? I'm not sure why but I thought Six might understand it. Wanted to ask her. Couldn't.

Her spiritual life is a mixture of her father's teachings, Christianity, and her own unique knowledge of things. She lives with a sense of integrity that puts most of us to shame. Yet she is a child. Her world is simpler. Compromise is still a new thing.

She has no notion of the force of attraction and longing. Any love she feels is pure and simple. On the ethics of dying, she knows very little, nor needs to know. These black holes are not for children.

Said nothing to her about all this. I searched for something that would console us both, but children hate it when you speak the obvious. I'd felt so tired, sitting here on this same bluff with her only minutes ago. The sinking sun, half hidden by cloud cover, had looked so foreboding. It burned behind the clouds like hot coals buried in ashes. Sometimes there's just too much to say.

She took us into the water. It did rejuvenate us. Six reminded me that it's movement that matters.

I don't know what to do about September or what to do with my feelings for Sloan. For Paul. It exhausts me just to think of them, but they are nearly all I think about.

Her hair is still dripping seawater down her neck when she reaches the cottage, shirtless with her notebook and pencil in hand. The warmth of the yellow light pouring from the bank of kitchen windows eases her shivering. What force of nature has pulled her here, she does not know.

After a few moments frozen in place, Claude feels the night air grow cooler yet. The wind sharpens and pushes her from behind toward the cottage. She walks around back to the screened door and opens it.

Here is the outdoor room where she had eaten the peaches and the chowder with Sloan. She walks to the next room where she finds music, Vivaldi and violins, and pockets of light that fall on a table, on an elaborate wicker chair, on a circle of pine flooring, on the murky drawings tacked to the walls. She takes it all in, this still life of the couple's life together.

She picks up a cotton throw that rests on the back of the wicker chair and wraps it around her. A strong aroma of seafood and thyme leads her to the kitchen. Here is the golden light she had seen from outside, and something about the room takes her back to another kitchen in another cottage, many years earlier. Everything looks familiar and safe and welcoming. She feels she's eaten many times at the porcelain enamel–topped table, knows its chipped surface, the faint blue elaborations on the edges, and the plain wooden legs. She tries to picture herself sitting there as a young girl, maybe her face is covered with rhubarb and strawberry pie. It could be late June. It could be Michigan.

There is a kettle, circled with spits of orangey dots, on the stovetop. She lights the flame beneath, as though she's done this here many times, and then raises the cast-iron lid. First comes the immediate hit of thyme, and then with a few swirls of a wooden spoon she finds lobster, shrimp, scallops, and chunks of potato and celery in a tomato broth. There are yellow pools of oil on the surface.

She removes her wet shorts and underwear and drapes them over a chair near the stove. She dries her hair with a kitchen towel and puts on the flannel shirt she finds hanging near the front door.

Claude sits at the table while the soup heats. Someone has placed there a clean bowl and spoon, a torn hunk of bread and bit of butter on a plate. A full glass of red wine is there, too, of such a deep red it is almost black. She takes a small sip. *Had they been expecting her?*

Claude ladles the soup into the bowl. She writes in her notebook and eats with the violins playing and all the comforting smells around her. She is intensely aware of but also oblivious to it all, as though she's sober and drunk at once. In a trance she writes and eats without stopping or haste. When the soup and bread are finished, she drinks the balance of the wine in the glass, feels it flush through her veins as she continues writing.

Then she covers the soup pot and places it in the refrigerator. She puts the bowl, spoon, and glass into a sink beautifully stained with a mosaic of past meals.

Claude walks back to the living room, the second room she had entered. This old cottage, she thinks, with its rattling windows and whispers of sea air, feels so lovingly tended and lived in. It is worn and sloppy, rich in the details of two complicated lives. She sees a telescope, collections of shells, pinecones, stones, and twisted scraps of beach wood. She touches a few spines of the books that are everywhere and runs her fingers over a long table's worn pine surface.

She can smell the fire now, the scent growing stronger as it loses intensity. She imagines Sloan building this fire for Paul to fend off this strangely cool August night.

Just to the left of the fireplace Claude sees the door that she knows will lead to a bedroom, as again she feels a rush of familiarity. She opens the door as though it is her own room she's entering. There are candles burning inside, shedding a dim light on a scene reminiscent of a fourteenth-century Dutch painting; it all seems dark and tragic, yet somehow alluring. Every corner of the room is blackened with only selected contours of objects touched by the light. A simple table. A ladderback chair piled with clothing. A rumpled rug. Bathed in the light of three pillar candles is an oak bed with a massive, ornately carved headboard. Paul is curled up in the center of the mattress. She sees the glimmer of sweat, his face crumpled with pain. He is shaking and his eyes are wide and staring into the darkness. He wears only a sleeveless undershirt and his briefs. Claude thinks of a brown worm curling on the sidewalk after a heavy rain; an unfortunate image but he looks that helpless.

Sloan's naked body is cupped around his backside. Her arms are curved around him, thick Picasso arms that bulge near the shoulders and then taper to the fingers in one continuous line.

Neither Paul nor Sloan acknowledges Claude's presence or the long stretch of time she stands there looking at them. A slap of sea air from a slightly opened window finally breaks her inertia, and she walks over to the bed. It is difficult for her to move, every step she takes violates reason, violates their intimacy. She removes her flannel shirt, picks up a sheet from the floor, and covers the two. Without thinking, Claude places her own warm, naked body down next to Paul's, her back to him. He slowly brings his hand to the curve of her hip. Moments later, Sloan's fingers reach a few strands of Claude's hair, and then rest on the nape of her neck.

The violins continue to labor through periods of vengeance and tranquility. Then they stop, as does Paul's trembling, with time. The three fall into a mindless comfort, blessed with the ease of sleeping alone.

GONE TO SEED

Paul gently raises his wife's arm and inches his way to the bottom of the crowded bed. He doesn't remember clearly how Claude came to join them. He stands up slowly, but then feels so lightheaded, he sits back down. He looks around his bedroom, sees the candle wax puddling on the floor near the open window. Again he tries standing and once he is up and stable, he blows out all the candles but one and closes the window.

He changes into his robe and a pair of sweatpants. His clothes feel like someone else's, a larger man's. The two women deep asleep in his bed also seem foreign to him. His mind flashes to Jesus at Gethsemane—now alone he must keep vigil over these last hours. He smiles, shakes his head, and leaves the room.

The fire has all but died, only a few embers and the orange lights from the stereo linger. He goes to the kitchen and sits at the table, pushing his back into the hard back of the chair. Paul sees that Claude has eaten; crumbs and splatters from the soup and wine cover the tabletop and the pages of an open notebook. He closes the book and drops it into the pocket of his robe. The wine bottle at his feet is empty, so he finds another on the counter and removes the cork. He pours an unhealthy amount into Claude's glass from the sink.

He takes a mouthful of the wine, holds it, and then swallows hard. And then again. There will be hell to pay for this indulgence, he knows, but right now his body needs the warmth and his mind, the blur.

Dying is a lonely job, he thinks. Even with all his father's showboating and his desire to take them all through it with him, he still had died alone, at the most forsaken hour of the night. Paul remembers being awake that night. He had noticed that the house had grown quiet, without his father's wheezing and hacking and his horrible moaning. No one ran to his bedside. He supposes now that they just had assumed it was over and went back to sleep. How odd, Paul now thinks. *Was that really how it happened?* And then there had followed the sparsely attended funeral. There had been no tears at all; he himself never cried for the man until years later.

After another slug of wine, Paul is visited by a memory of his grandmother so vivid that it seems to bring her into the room with him. He remembers presenting her with a drawing he had made of God, a figure with the usual yellow ring over the head; but his God had been black and a woman with long, thick hair and a full bosom. It had been crudely drawn with no clouds or background, but it had made his grandmother cry. He remembers her wiping away tears with the narrow ties of her apron. It surprises him now how well he can picture that pretty apron—the checkered edges, the pastel flowers, always so clean as though she had just put it on fresh. The old woman had pulled his face to her breasts, and he had heard her heart and her words blend into something like an African chant as she cried and spoke. "It's so beautiful, boy, I have t'cry t'let it out." *What did she see in that picture?* And then it comes to him here in his own kitchen so many years later. She had seen herself in that picture as Paul had needed her to be, as his religion, his security, the known and predictable in his small life.

And then, just as quickly as she had appeared, the ghost leaves the room. In her wake is left only sadness and fatigue. Now Paul craves only sleep, a deep sleep, a long and mindless sleep. There's another name for that, he thinks, and again, he drinks from the bottle and his stomach tightens.

He picks up a crumpled, brown bag from the floor. "Ah, the wine's sheath. Perfect for my last words," he says.

Utilizing Claude's dulled pencil, he composes this line:

It's true, I have been abandoned by my own body

"All right then," he exhales, but he feels a little nugget of fear creeping into his thoughts. He thinks perhaps another slug will dislodge other, more hopeful lines:

but when the sun rises on the beach and falls on the shell that was my body,
those bones that held me upright and those that protected my thoughts,
there will also rise above that shell a shimmering, well-dressed other self
a self in a suit far finer than my income, showy, more Vegas than me

a bigger, more boisterous, wiser, with better jokes kind of self,
and then the hungry tide can have my corpse

Pretty depressing, he thinks. *What the hell is a shimmering, well-dressed other self?* The first light of dawn is now on the horizon. He continues:

I gladly return this body to the tide to decompose,
to be divinely ordered to better purpose

"It's a bit wordy for an epitaph," he whispers. "But one last line."

Because all that I am is none of that

And with that bit of brilliance, he hurries to the bathroom. Once his system has emptied out, he goes to the couch and wraps a blanket around his shaking body. "I hate this dying," he says. "There are no surprise endings."

He curls into the couch and pulls Claude's notebook from his pocket. Paul randomly reads about a woman's obsession with light and with his wife. This same man in a different time and situation would not have violated her right to privacy. It was one thing to expose her photographs without asking, but to pry into her private thoughts, he knows this to be truly unethical. But he forces himself to read on, not out of curiosity, because it is painful to read this testimonial. He must know if she feels anything authentic, anything lasting, anything at all for Sloan.

It is uncomfortable for Sonny to see Barton awash in the fluorescent light of White's Hardware. Barton looks green and raw and like he's been through one more thing than he can handle. Sonny's first impulse is to pretend he doesn't see him at all. But then, there amidst the nails and screws with his hands full of tidy little boxes, Barton looks straight at him.

"I'm building a picnic table for Cherry," Barton says.

Well, thinks Sonny, that explains why you were fucking my wife and sleeping on my couch in my own fucking shorts. But then he smiles, feels some compassion, as is his nature. He puts down his toilet plunger and takes a box from Barton's stack. "These won't be long enough if you're going through a two by six." Then he runs his finger down the shelf of exterior screws until he sees what he wants.

"I'd use these three-inchers. They come with a bit, too. Of course, you'll need carriage bolts, too."

Sonny puts the box on top of the others in Barton's hands. "Stay away from my wife," he tells him. "It ain't natural."

Then Sonny turns away and throws his plunger over his shoulder as if it were a weapon. He finds himself wishing it could have been at least a plumber's wrench.

August 27

Watched the cars arrive from my outpost on the bluff. They all drove right by the fee box after the briefest of stops. I should have cared but I was busy waiting.

It was almost noon when they appeared. Sloan carried an old wicker laundry basket on her head. I felt some weird ancient yearning deep in my gut, as if she was returning to me from the river's edge with our freshly washed clothing.

Paul labored through his steps, wrapped in a lightweight red blanket even in the heat. He wouldn't look at me. After our night together, I'd left him sleeping on the couch. My journal was on the table next to him. If he'd read even a few pages, he'd have reason to distrust me, pity me, or both.

But there's nothing in it he doesn't already know.

We walked to the nearest cove east, to the small group of birches above the beach. Climbed into the hollow between the trunks. Sloan laid a white linen tablecloth on the ground.

Paul announced that the food was from last night's menu, the last meal of the season at the Spiritoso. Glazed duck, wild rice, string beans with almonds, and a fruit salad that was struggling. And then, dinner plates as immaculate as Sister Yvonne's souls appeared and a Fumé Blanc that Paul proclaimed the perfect late-morning wine. He handed me a cloth napkin, scented with the incense-like fragrance of the restaurant. Where were the candles and the chalice?

We ate in the usual fashion, Paul abstaining, and Sloan and I shoveling food into our mouths. And then the last ritual, the sacrifice. I was placed on my back on that same linen cloth over a mattress of sand and decomposing leaves. With the sweet fragrance of the wine on her breath, Sloan bent low to undress me and then stood to remove her own clothing. Paul was close, sitting cross-legged behind my head, his red blanket touching my cheek.

She brought the full weight of her body against me. I could feel every grain of sand and bit of twig beneath me. I squirmed. I just wasn't interested this time. I was about to ask her to stop, but she rose up and slid her body up and down against mine. I believe she may have kissed Paul once or twice. I changed my mind, maybe as much for his small involvement as hers. Paul drew my arms toward him and stroked repeatedly from the inside of my wrist to the tenderness in the underbelly of my elbow. His gentleness, this sweet attention, intensified the force of her movements.

She was at her most creative and it must have been exhausting for him to even watch this. When he sensed my urgency, he firmly held my wrists in place over my head while the pulsing pressure of her clitoris against my own drove me to a state of complete insanity. And once I remembered to breathe again, he had let loose my wrists and I found that they were burning and that her lips were on his.

I cried. I knew this was to be the last time. I began to shake uncontrollably and Paul recovered the tablecloth that had been kicked aside. He shook the debris away and laid it over me, fatherly.

Someone could easily have seen all this. It would be an interesting addition to the family video. But we felt alone in the world, Adam, Eve, and Claude. I think we all felt this separation from the rest of the world, an intense loneliness together. Paul wrapped his naked wife in his blanket and we all slept for a while in the cooler shade as the August heat intensified.

When I woke, they were gone and all their ceremonial implements had vanished. Even the impressions of their bodies were blown clean away.

I just picked up 157 cigarette butts from the parking lot, even those hiding beneath the gravel. Found thirty-seven cents. The parking lot is empty and there are five dollar bills stuffed into the fee box.

Darkness is a long time coming.

I do understand. I will try to forgive them for infusing this uncertainty into my life, for stealing from me my love of solitude and offering only a bleak loneliness in return. In a way though, all the unpredictability is liberating. It makes the urge to plan tomorrow or any of my life so ridiculous.

SEPTEMBER 2001

HOW CAN YOU KNOW
IF WHAT YOU WITNESS
IS REAL OR IMAGINARY?
WHAT PROOF CAN YOU MUSTER
WHEN WRITING ONLY WITH LIGHT IN DARKNESS?

Cherry had pedaled all the way to the Floyd Library in Greenport to research various herbs she hoped would strengthen Paul's immune system. She had assembled a list of potent remedies for everything from irritated bowels to cancer to AIDS. Then she had journeyed to the natural food market on Front Street where she filled small brown paper bags with a dozen different ingredients. Each sack had been neatly labeled with its contents using a fine-point marking pen, and then had been tossed into her canvas backpack for the journey home. Had it not been for the unexpected downpour on her return trip to Orient, St.-John's-wort would have been easily distinguishable from wahoo bark, and red clover from kava kava.

Cherry then had been forced to sprinkle these innominate remedies randomly into her mother's zucchini bread recipe, relying on divine providence to provide for Paul those herbs most beneficial. Now she presents the loaf with the green, bitter clumps to Paul, but he can barely choke down the smallest of bites.

"You look like death with a hangover," she tells him, "so you better eat this whole damn thing." Paul laughs, and with eyes tearing proclaims, "It's perfectly delicious. Perfect in every way."

When she rides her bicycle back to her trailer, it is nearly nightfall and the rain has stopped. Cherry contemplates Paul's reaction to her gift, and how akin laughter is to crying. Some small switch deep within the brain triggers one or the other, sometimes provoking the one which seems most inappropriate, like when she had broken into uncontrollable laughter at her mother's funeral. She was truly sad and hadn't meant to be mean, but it must have looked that way to the elderly Polish ladies in attendance. Not that they hadn't already been horrified to see the missing son now returned in a little black dress and heels of an inappropriate height for a funeral.

And sometimes, too, she realizes as she gets closer to home, anger can make love look a lot like rage. She hates coming back to the empty trailer, hates sleeping alone, but at that moment she can't quite remember if she had asked Barton to leave or it had been his idea. Maybe it just happened because the exact number of days they were to spend together had been reached. Sometimes it's an illness that determines this number. Sometimes it's an infidelity or a silly misunderstanding. Somehow, the number of days is reached and it's over. Cherry is sad to admit it, but it could be that simple. But then she senses a shimmer of hopefulness, a glimmer of light that breaks the dismal horizon. Maybe time could be her friend. A specific amount of time might determine when forgiveness is possible.

Not as dramatic, but just as likely.

September 1

It has been days, but when I did see Paul today, what I saw first was his diminishing, what was not there. If he does take his own life, he'll only be able to take what's left.

Our beach walk this afternoon was short, the pace slow and meandering. There was nothing to eat and Sloan and I never touched each other.

I suppose my work is done.

It's as if we're all half-wittedly paddling the calm stretch of the river before it trips into the falls. These days will pass slowly as we all watch his soul gradually gain dominance, breaking through the meager confines of his material self.

LAST SUPPERS

BUT HOPE THAT IS SEEN IS NOT HOPE.
FOR HOW CAN A MAN HOPE FOR WHAT HE SEES?
BUT IF WE HOPE FOR WHAT WE DO NOT SEE,
WE WAIT FOR IT WITH PATIENCE.

Romans 8:24-25

The last bit of summer has been quiet and enough on the fringe of normal to make normal seem poignant. Oddly cool temperatures, more heavy rains, and a tedious, offshore wind are spoiling the holiday weekend for the summer people, but making it all the sweeter for the locals. The roads are empty, the beaches deserted, the markets manageable.

Claude has been hiding away in her booth, often sleeping on the floor, sometimes reading by the orange glow of an electric heater. She is relying on a diverse collection of books to advise her solitude. There is Moore's *The Re-enchantment of Everyday Life,* and books of poetry by Donald Hall, Philip Levine, and Mark Doty. She studies obsession in *Lolita* and in the Bible, and throws in some short stories by Hemingway just for the comfort of being somewhere else. She jumps from book to book as though cramming for finals. Strips of paper mark passages. Take-out containers litter the floor, a particularly dark indication of Claude's state of mind. Very little makes its way into her journal.

The early closing of the Spiritoso has been hard on Cherry. Even though Barton still sleeps in his workshop, she feels compelled to bring him supper, as she does for Saugerties. She is forced to rely on her own imagination and skills in preparing these meals, which have produced creative but often inedible dishes. Barton feels he deserves the mistreatment, and Saugerties would eat a shoe if you cut it into small enough pieces. On the nights of the most obvious failures, the Blue Light is utilized.

Paul continues to cook in his own beachfront kitchen as best he can. The dishes are simple...roasted chickens, salads, plates of fruit and cheeses. Most of the food is either given or thrown away. Sloan has learned to pay the bills, and it seems as if the couple is often on the cusp of an argument that neither has the energy to pursue. Equal parts of calamity and futility have resulted in the worrisome but loving melancholy that permeates their cottage.

On this third day of September, Paul and Sloan are spending the morning perfecting his classic bread. They blend whole-grain and unbleached white flours to create the perfectly dense yet porous texture. After the dough has risen, they roll into the yeasty mix diced calamata olives, sun-dried tomatoes, rosemary, and a tangy havarti. It smells so tantalizing as it bakes, Paul tells her that the aroma alone will be sustenance enough for him.

While the bread continues to bake and the rain comes down once more, they sit at the kitchen table by the window. They become mesmerized by the blades and plumes of the tall grasses outside in their heady dance with the rain and the wind. Paul stares at the determined beads of water clinging to the tiny seed pods of the switch grass. The effort seems so futile that it makes it all the more lovely to him. He rests his hand lightly on his wife's.

And then, with windows rattling and the *tah-tah-tah* of hard bits of rain on the roof, they kiss and then kiss again They share brief touches on lips and longer, moist, open-mouthed kisses. Across the small table, they speak briefly of their past and their awkward romance. They laugh at themselves. Fingertips touch forearms or circle a mouth. All these touches are void of passion. At this moment in their life together, touch is more akin to love than to lovemaking.

In time, Paul removes the bread from the oven with great reverence and places it on the table. They curve their palms around the loaf to feel the warmth it exhales. Paul remarks that he understands why Jesus chose to break bread with his disciples at their last meal together. "Bread is intended more to feed the soul than to feed the body," he says to his wife.

That evening they sit on bed pillows by the fire, on those same yellowed pillows with the blue ticking from Sloan's past. They feed small pieces of the bread to each other. Miles Davis' *Kind of Blue* punctuates their simple meal, as Paul had been craving the whispered assurances of the trumpeter. Miles will be the angel at heaven's gate, he tells his wife, an angel far more joyous than blue.

But for Sloan, the music is thick and confusing and unbearably sad. She drinks an entire bottle of wine in measured sips as they watch the fire, and then she falls asleep with her heavy head resting on her husband's thigh.

September 3

One more visit tonight.

She barged in and filled the small room with the darkness and the storm and her wild, panicked eyes. I jumped to my feet fearing I would have to defend myself. She was soaked and there was a sour, fermented smell to her.

Got the blanket from my chair, but she gripped my arm as I was about to wrap it around her. She pulled me into her wet body and I felt the shaking. She began to pull at my clothes, still with that crazed look in her eyes. I tried to talk to her, ask her what was wrong.

She pulled away and handed me a plastic bag. Inside was a soggy mass, bread I suppose it once was, with chunks of red and black buried in it. She said in a complete monotone that she was sorry, said it two or three times. I don't know if it was for the mush in the bag or for the mess of the entire summer. Probably the mush.

I had already let her go, and Paul as well. Had found some distance. But when she began to run her hands under my shirt, I started losing ground. I stopped her frantic pawing, and pulled her wet shirt over her head and took off her wet trousers and underwear. She looked a lot less formidable once naked. She pulled me into her again and I pressed my mouth on hers. She abruptly turned her face into my neck, but not in a mean way, more to hide.

On the blanket on the floor where I have spent so many hours trying to dream her away, dream them both away, we made love or as close to that as we've ever been. At least I felt that she was really there, even if it was out of desperation.

Pleasure and pain. You can't feel them both at the same time.

Once it was over, I stayed there with her for awhile listening to the sound of the electric heater, humming along in the most ordinary way. I knew that the stunned creature allowing me to hold her would soon be scurrying back to her lair. To her husband. Knew that her pain would return. I got up and dressed as she stared at the ceiling. Before I left, I stood above her and told her to take the blanket with her and that I would be there on Friday at dawn. I told her everything would be all right. That's what you say. She said nothing, never even looked at me.

She's gone now. Came back and found the blanket still on the floor, her underwear left in a dark corner.

Of course, I don't know how it will be, after he knocks back his pentobarbital with a glass of good wine. I know his respiration will drop, but just how long will it be before he pulls his last breath? Will we talk while we wait? God, I hope not.

And what do we do with his body after he dies? Should we carry him home, or bury him under the pines, or call a mortician? Do we tell the truth to the police? I suppose we will be considered accomplices. Or worse.

And what if it rains Friday as it has all day today? Can a suicide have a rain date?

And then, after all that, there's the night to face and the next day and the next. How many nights and how many dreams will it take to blur the horrific details of these next few days?

September 4

Tomorrow I'll return all my books. Life just isn't a string of neat little paragraphs, one leading logically to the next. So goodbye sweet Lolita and farewell St. Paul, the beloved. Both describe to me different forms of craving and broken faith. Donald Hall's "Without," so full of love and longing, is primarily about loss, the shocking sticker price of any happiness.

Writing is for the benefit of the writer anyway. Readers are only secondary concerns. This journal is proof of that.

I'll only keep my books on horticulture. I'll line these shelves with hard little facts on organic fertilizers, plant diseases, proper pruning, and botanical names fashioned in a predictable, dead language. I need to know that one never plants gooseberry bushes near Pinus strobus because of the deadly blister rust. Raw fish not only contains all the major and minor nutrients in spades, but also is a reliable bacteria stimulator which speeds up the breakdown of organic matter into humus. But never, ever allow the raw fish to come in contact with plant roots. Work it into trenches in the fall or bury it deep in the compost pile. Wet seaweed contains a bit more nitrogen than stable manure and twice as much potash.

These are facts, neat and true. There are facts, too, on human decomposition. What exactly is the nutrient and soil-conditioning value of the human body as it reintegrates with the earth? What exactly is the denial we foster when we purchase liners and vaults for our loved ones when they die?

Whether or not suicide eternally stains the soul is no concern of mine. I'm just a midwife at this reverse birth and have nothing to say about the right to die or death rites or the legitimacy of the whole thing.

THE RACKET OF LIFE

Claude is horrified to see that Arthur has sold Six's paperback Bible to Lenny's bookstore. There it is on his outdoor table, tattered and wearing a fifty-cents sticker. She finds both their names inscribed in Six's pen on the title page.

To have seen Sonny in the arms of a nun would have shocked her less. The betrayal seems enormous. She buys it back and takes it down to the pier. With feet dangling, she sits with this precious thing in her hands. As she flips through the book she discovers that Six has personalized the text. There are little drawings, mostly faces and upper torsos. Animals, angels, saints, Christ Himself...Claude is not sure about their identities, but they are simple and beautiful and reminiscent of the Mexican painter Tamayo, primitive and powerfully evocative. And, of course, there are underlined and highlighted passages, as well as food stains and a few torn pages. She knows that this beloved book has been her companion for years. It even smells like her.

Claude finds that the Bible opens naturally to Leviticus 26 where verse 15 is underlined with a bold pen:

IF YOU REFUSE TO OBEY MY LAWS AND COMMANDS
AND BREAK THE COVENANT I HAVE MADE WITH YOU,
I WILL PUNISH YOU. I WILL BRING DISASTER ON YOU—
INCURABLE DISEASE AND FEVERS THAT WILL MAKE YOU BLIND
AND CAUSE YOUR LIFE TO WASTE AWAY.

Claude thinks of Rae and the plight that may lie before her, at least in the eyes of God and Six. She also worries about her own actions in this dismal context. She then seeks out another easy opening of the book and finds, with squiggly lines radiating from the passage, this piece of the 46th Psalm:

GOD IS OUR SHELTER AND STRENGTH,
ALWAYS READY TO HELP IN TIMES OF TROUBLE.
SO WE WILL NOT BE AFRAID, EVEN IF THE EARTH IS SHAKEN
AND MOUNTAINS FALL INTO THE OCEAN'S DEPTHS;
EVEN IF THE SEAS ROAR AND RAGE

Comforted, Claude sits there on the pier for some time holding the book close to her chest, with all the racket of life around her...the screaming gulls, the children's begging voices, the throbbing car stereos, and the knocking of rigging against mast. As best she can, she prays to Six's God not for resolution but for His presence, for tangible, measurable grace. And she prays for Paul. And, of course, most fervently for Six.

September 5

We must all seem like heathens to Six, nonbelievers, conjurers of the worst sort, making up our own individual moralities as we go along.

There was a time I didn't believe at all. I became deeply disillusioned with the religion I grew up with. It seemed to foster feelings of superiority and intolerance. If there was a heaven, I was convinced at an early age that there were not penthouses for us Catholics and cots in the laundry room for all the unbaptized. Christ would never be that sort of concierge.

I so want to believe in God. I do believe in this nine-year-old girl, still fresh enough from her before-life to remember what really matters. What would children tell us if we weren't always telling them what to say, what to think, how to behave, and what to believe?

Six challenges me to think with the simple mind of a child again, about God, and the purity of soul and intention. Soul to her is not an empty circle that serves as your spiritual report card. Soul to her is not Aretha's singing, but the energy in it that moves you, moves you to dance wildly or be wildly happy or to swim at night. I do feel God in this girl, as I feel God in the vastness of the ocean or the intricacies of nature. There's something pure here. Pure. What a beautiful word, pure. Put it in front of any noun and it gives that word new depth of meaning. Pure love. Pure grief. Pure spirit. Pure fantasy?

I've read that God is not the ocean, but the waves in the ocean. God is process, not personality. Not an entity, but entirety.

All religions say in one way or another that God is ultimately love, which is the best thing in us, maybe all that is eternal. God demands sacrifice. Sacrifice for love, which is the core message of the greatest act of love in Christian belief.

We seem to shy away from declaring our religious preferences and beliefs about God. It makes us uncomfortable. But why? I'm sure we're not born with this discomfort. We seem to learn this with age. And then once we're truly old, or threatened with an early death, it seems talk of God becomes permissible once again. How strange.

I hope for Paul that there is a loving God present for him on Friday, the God of the New Testament not the Old, not the vindictive, angry God. And that His grace will provide the cleansing forgetfulness to ease the transition between life and death as it does between death and life.

A STALE CLOUD OF BEER VAPOR

Paul comes late that last night, around one, to Sonny's place. Rae is working; it is just a typical Thursday night for them. Six had stayed up late with Sonny, even though it was a school night. Her mother had voiced strong objections before she left, but he had insisted. "We can't just back out this late in the game," he had told her. "Besides, she'd still be listening even if she was in bed."

Then later, Paul's urgent knockings wake Sonny from a deep sleep. He appears, half-dazed, at the trailer door, wearing only a pair of shiny gold boxers slung beneath his belly. With the kitchen light glowing behind him, he looks to Paul like some bronzed Aztec chieftain.

"What the hell is it, Paul? You okay?"

As the night noises increase in volume, Paul can't seem to remember why he's come. Sonny's eyes close as though he might return to sleep standing there. Paul wonders if he's sober. He focuses on the chieftain and then realizes that Sonny might fall forward and transubstantiate his frail self into a pile of mostly clothes. Time to speak, Paul scolds himself. *Say something. Anything.*

"I'd...like or I...need to talk to you, man. I mean, if you have a few minutes. Maybe we could sit there." Here he points at the room behind Sonny, as though he might have some trouble locating his own kitchen. "It won't take long."

Sonny says nothing, only twists his body in the opposite direction and stumbles into the kitchen. He lowers himself into a chair.

Paul steps into their home; he has never been inside. The place smells of salt, as from bacon or popcorn. It is not unpleasant, but a comforting and familiar aroma, like that of an old movie theater. The décor is pure, unabashed *Rae*. All reds and golds, flocked wallpaper, and a glitzy mirror which Paul is certain outweighs him. *Has he stumbled into a Tennessee whorehouse?* Dishes are piled high in the sink and Budweiser cans form a small metropolis on the stovetop. He sits across the kitchen table from Sonny and tries to compose his thoughts.

"Sonny...I believe you are a wise man. I'm not sure how I know that, but..." Sonny looks confused and is growing impatient. Paul stammers on, "but could you tell me what you know about dying? Well, both the dying part...and after that..."

This wakes him up. He fixes his watery eyes on Paul. "You do look like shit, man."

"Well, thanks. I hadn't realized." Paul is gaining a little momentum now. "You know, I've been sort of avoiding the mirror lately. I have pancreatic cancer. Or it has me. I don't want any medical intervention, since they've promised me little help anyway, only a little more time, which I would be too sick to appreciate. So my time's pretty much up now. I feel it. My eyes are yellow and my urine is as dark as lager." Sonny winces and screws up his face. His hand comes up to block the details he fears are coming. Paul continues nevertheless. "Poison is building in my blood. The nerves in my back are screaming from the pain caused by the pressure of the tumor. I can't eat. I can't cook. I can't even make love to my wife."

Sonny remembers the weird scene on the beach, seeing the two women together and Paul's awkward reaction to it. He runs both his hands through his long, black hair and raises his face toward the garish light source above him. His face is really remarkable, Paul thinks. He can see the fine lines of his ancestry etched into his beautiful skin. His eyes are as black as a midwinter night, with irises as clear as the North Star in that blackness. Paul admires the ridge of his high cheekbones and the plummeting, broad plains that fall beneath. *Has he ever seen such majesty in a face?* He feels delirious.

Finally, Sonny brings his eyes to Paul's. Sonny still looks dazed, but profoundly dazed, bearing the gaze of a mystic or a monk. His mouth opens and there emerges from the depths of his being a stale cloud of yeasty vapor, and then he asks, "Wanna beer?"

Paul is disappointed and now uses what little strength he has to mount an angry response. "Have you been listening to me at all, man? I'm ready to check myself out. Tomorrow! You know, as in a few hours. When the sun rises..." He pauses and then in a muffled scream, "I'm outta here!"

Sonny jumps from his seat and pushes his palms repeatedly toward the tabletop. "Keep it down, man, keep it down. Six is sleeping. She's got school."

Sonny then walks to his refrigerator, finds two cans of beer and brings them ceremoniously to the table. Paul is quiet now. He finds the sharp rip of the opening of the cans annoying, as is Sonny's silence as they drink. The smell of the beer makes Paul gag, but he still pours it down his throat. It is surprisingly good, cold and neat. As he drinks, he remembers Sloan, sees her naked, knotted up in their top sheet. Feels himself both there, and here.

Just before his final chug, Sonny's face begins to twitch and he looks straight at his drinking companion for a moment or two. Then his entire body becomes motionless except for his mouth. "Die under the open sky. Do it in such a way as respects your family, especially those who are gone." A quick burp jolts him and then Sonny's entire body starts to quiver. His next words come quickly, as though the words are burning his tongue and he must spit them out. "Don't be afraid. You will exhale in this world and inhale in the next. Death will come that fast. Remain calm. If you see death as a battle, it'll be difficult for you, and you'll lose anyway. You must surrender willingly to it."

He pauses before continuing, holding Paul in his seat with his relentless stare. "Remain calm," he repeats. "A warm wind will find you and carry you safely away, carry you like a child in the arms of your grandmother."

Paul is immobilized by the weight of Sonny's words; they seem to have shape and linger in the space between them. *How did he know about her?* He doesn't want to finish his beer but he does so just to move, to have something to do. Then he stands up in the cramped kitchen space. The faux walnut veneer and gold-speckled Formica disappear and he feels as though he is floating above a fragile earth, his head rising into the cold, light air of the troposphere. He can see nothing clearly but everything in abstraction from this distance. His eyes finally drift down to Sonny, who has made a pillow of his forearms and seems fast asleep. Paul bends low and places his right palm on that silken head. "Thank you, Chief. I love you, man."

Before Paul leaves the mobile home, he rouses Sonny enough to coax him back to bed. Once there, he draws a sheet to his chin.

"Will you even remember that I was here?" Paul says, as he eases the aluminum door closed behind him.

AN ODD FLICKER OF LIGHT

Sleep had always been a mindless safe haven for her, but for weeks now Sloan hasn't slept well at all. Her formerly dreamless nights are now riddled with dreams that confuse and exhaust her. This night after she hears Paul leave the cottage, she rises from her feigned sleep, goes to Paul's top drawer and then to the kitchen. By the light of a single candle, Sloan opens the box of poems. Sitting on top of the pile inside is a crumpled menu, and on the back are words written in Paul's tight, square printing. She knows that the little that can be said, has been said. Still, it is better to read this now than after:

> So then here I go with a child's lack of fear
> into the night
>
> I'll wrap my body in a white sail
> fly with the wind fast and high and
> my love, from the beach you will witness
> a distant, odd flicker of light
> against the murky night sky
>
> That's my small sail
> dazzling like a skate's blade
> in the sharp winter sun
> you see but pay little mind
> the night is growing deep
> and you are fighting sleep

Sloan looks away from the paper. She stares at the dark corners of the room until soft details emerge from the blackness. What a silly jumble of words, she thinks. Anyway, it is sleep that is fighting her, not the other way around. She forces down the last lines:

> By daylight so insignificant am I
> just a tiny bit of the everything you see
> but I will force your smile
> a smile of easy contentment
> as you catch once again my tiny flit of sailcloth
> in the vast blues of water and sky
>
> You'll pause to think of me
> without even knowing why

Sloan can't follow his meaning, but she knows if this thing had been written to make her feel better, it failed. The words look to her like crumbs on the paper. *A sail? A skate? What is he talking about?* She throws the menu into the wastebasket beneath the sink, where it quickly absorbs liquids from the night's uneaten dinner.

Thirty minutes later, she leaves her bed for the second time and is back beneath the sink. She exhumes the menu, gently rinses it, and places it between two paper towels. She returns to bed and listens to the wind lifting the old cedar shake of their cottage, piece by piece, in a musical flapping that makes her solitude quite frightening.

September 7

The sun is due up soon. I will go as I said I would.

I wonder what tonight will be like. And what will we be preoccupied with at the end of September? What about during the third week of October? What will it be like when Sonny puts the turkey on the table for us at Thanksgiving? What will our prayers of gratitude encompass?

I remember a morning just before dawn last autumn when I was sitting beneath a maple tree near the train station in Greenport. Her broad leaves were of a butterscotch color, brilliant even in the near darkness. I sat there, listening to the petioles tearing from the twigs and the listless falling through air, then the soft and perfect landing of each leaf. That last sound like a sigh, that light and that long. Over and over again, the tearing, the slicing through air, the sighing. I never boarded the train.

Why this stays with me, I don't know, but it is such a clear, sad recollection, like time spent with close friends after a funeral.

The funeral. Will there even be one?

FIRST FRIDAY

IN THE BEGINNING, GOD CREATED HEAVEN AND EARTH.
AND THE EARTH WAS FORMLESS AND EMPTY.
THE RAGGED OCEAN THAT COVERED EVERYTHING
WAS ENGULFED IN TOTAL DARKNESS,
AND THE POWER OF GOD MOVED OVER THE WATERS.
THEN GOD COMMANDED, "LET THERE BE LIGHT"
—AND LIGHT APPEARED.

Genesis 1:1-3

On this first Friday in September, they have met east of the county park on a solemn stretch of beach. The sun is still low and apprehensive on the horizon. Paul feels its hesitation, but he experiences none of it himself. He had asked Sloan and Claude to wear white, and they are in white t-shirts, clean and awash in the hues of the sun's earliest light. He is naked, draped only in his perfect, gilded skin and curled into the sand on his side, his knees drawn to his chest. His head rests in his wife's hands. Both face east. Off to the side sits Claude, watching the small wave crests as they ease to shore, each tiny wave still dressed in night's somber colors. She has promised herself she will stay safely in the visual plane. She allows no thoughts, no feelings; she is as objective as a juror.

The wind comes in weak sighs. Summer has returned but as a sweet mix of moderate temperature and low humidity.

To Paul, there is nothing left to be said or done, only the dying. In the sand is the vial of pentobarbital, 40 capsules, 100 milliliters each. He knows it will take a while to get them down. Then there will come the drop in respiration, the anesthetizing effects. The pills are courtesy— it was so easily done—of a friend of a friend of a veterinarian. Next to the vial, a bottle of Reserve Merlot. The wine is ceremonial; water will be used to swallow the pills. By midmorning at least, he hopes to be with her, in the arms of the other woman in his life. It could be that simple, that love endures even past the last breath. Or, he must acknowledge, it could be something else entirely.

Sloan had not slept. She had been awake when he left in the middle of the night, and awake once he had returned. It was then that she had tried to coax him from his resolve. "Why not another day?" she'd asked. She had pleaded to spend one more day together, just the two of them, just one more day. But he would hear none of it. He was "packed and ready," he had announced. She had said nothing else, not then, and not on the slow walk to this spot on the beach at dawn.

He has planned his dying to be like his birth, again naked and in the presence of water. But this time, not in his grandmother's bedroom with shouts of pain from a teenage mother. No, he is out under the open sky, as Sonny had instructed. And yes, Paul knows, there will be some pain in this process as well. But then no more.

Paul had asked that Claude read from the Book of Genesis, and she has with her this morning Six's ravaged Bible. He had realized that she would need something very specific to occupy her, so she is to begin reading when he begins swallowing the pills, and continue reading until he is, as he put it, "delivered."

Now ready and willing to die, he lingers a moment more. He waits for the sun to fully reveal itself, to step forward as a witness to his passing. But then, there, flat against the earth and curled like a fetus, he soon realizes that he has not thought of everything.

A BRITTLE SNAP

DO ME JUSTICE, O LORD,
FOR I HAVE WALKED IN MY INNOCENCE,
AND HAVING TRUSTED IN THE LORD,
I HAVE NOT WAVERED.

Psalms 25:1

She's running, jumping stumps, and flying like a forest native. Though barefoot, she doesn't slip on the dewy bed of pine needles. She ducks under low, fingering branches. The path's so soft, she must be light-footed to get up good speed. She leaves barely an imprint. Determined footfalls land again and again, guided only by knowledge of terrain and the weak morning light.

Now there's only sand squeezing between her toes, a relief from the needles and cones. She relishes the small climb to the backside of the bluff, enjoys the pull on her calves. It's as easy for her as a downhill romp. More running, now along the bluff. Here and there she loses her footing and must regain her speed. The intoxicating scent of sea and purpose seep into her pores. It almost seems to her as if it's already done.

Faces flash in her mind. Arthur, still half asleep, dreading the third day of school. And then, Claude, red in the face from talking and talking. And Rae. She will not think of her mother right now. But then comes the face of her father—full of pride and stubble and the right understanding of things. Her love for him is as tangible as what she carries in her hands. He will understand.

But now she must wash away these faces and focus on but one. She stops. She's found him. She quiets her breathing and sharpens her focus. He's there with them, on the beach below. She nestles the Winchester and squints to make him the size and importance of only a beer can. Steadying for the kickback, she braces and eases the trigger toward her.

A brittle snap, sudden and clean. Just one shot.

All heads swing in the direction of the noise. Then for a few slow seconds of lavish disbelief, they stare hard at the bluff where a girl regains her stance and drops the rifle's butt to the sand.

Paul's right hand goes to the wound on his left side. Sloan pulls off her shirt and tries to press it against the curve of his rib cage, but his hand weakly keeps pushing hers away. He then leans into her and rests his head against her bare breasts. He redirects his eyes to the child and holds her fixed on the bluff. "It's all right," he says. A pause, and then the beginning of Sloan's crying. "It's all right," he whispers to her and closes his hand around his wife's wrist.

Claude's eyes travel from the child to Paul and then to the Bible she has dropped at her feet. She can't decide whether to go to Paul or up the bluff to Six, so is unable to move in either direction.

Claude looks at Sloan who is holding her husband's head tight against her. She is moaning and crying. His eyes are still locked with the girl's. *How much time has passed?* Claude sees his lips, his beautiful lips as sweet as a child's, curling in pure what? *Is it love? Forgiveness? Gratitude?* Blood eases from his side into the sand, never pooling, but painting a lush stain that grows darker as it reaches greater depth. This is a dream, Claude realizes, and smiles with relief. Free now to enjoy the dream's imagery, she watches as his blood pours like spilled wine and soaks deeper yet into the sand. The earth seems thirsty, she observes with a smile, as though it can't pull the blood from him fast enough.

But then she sees Sonny, running hard on the beach, coming from the east. His eyes scan the scene as he runs, assessing, and then finally rest on his daughter on the bluff. He is still in his boxer shorts, his chest wet with sweat. He scrambles up the bluff, taking it in a series of grabbing lurches with hands and feet. His eyes stay on his daughter who still stands there, the rifle's barrel in one hand. Once Sonny reaches her, in a single, liquid motion, he cups the barrel of the weapon and pulls it away, while his free arm encircles his daughter's head. He draws her to him. Her small frame is rigid but trembling. Sonny lets go of her long enough to wipe down the entire rifle with the loose fabric of his shorts. While working, he sees his wife running towards the figures below, her hands flipping at her sides like tiny, ineffectual wings.

Sonny gathers his daughter into his arms, and then carries her and his rifle toward home. She seems so heavy to him, so weighed down with what she's done. She is limp and appears to be asleep before they even reach the woods. He cannot get Paul's angry face from his mind. He sees him there in his kitchen, wide-eyed and demanding. As he carries Six into the trailer park, he hears again Paul's loud declaration from the night before, "I'm outta here!"

And as he lowers her into her bed, he feels a weakness in his knees. He falls into her messy lair and curls his body around his daughter. "Why? Why? Why?" he keeps whispering to her, and to himself, and to what he perceives at that moment to be a sprawling, very fucked-up universe.

Rae catches a glimpse of Six and Sonny as they disappear into the pines. She'd left work a little early, hadn't felt right. Now she knows why. Her family had been missing when she came home, and then she'd heard the pop. Now she stands still for a moment, sinking into the sand, her heart racing. She keeps looking from the bluff to Paul and back again. Thoughts come in gulps. Something is missing, she thinks, something like reality. She walks quickly to Paul, bends down, and pulls the now red shirt away from his wound. *Where are the rest of his clothes?*

"What the bloody hell happened? Did Sonny shoot him? Did Six see any of this?" She blurts out these things, each word louder than the one before. No one answers.

She pushes Sloan aside, seeing for the first time that her breasts are exposed. Rae knows she is certainly missing something, but this will have to be sorted out later. She examines the wound as best she can. "Paul, calm down. You'll be all right. Claude, for God's sake, go call an ambulance." But no one moves.

Rae's face reddens. She is losing all patience. Now her jutting lips form each word with great theatricality. "What the fuck is wrong with you? He needs a doctor. I can slow the blood loss, but..."

Paul interrupts. "I don't need a doctor, Rae." And then, very weakly, "I'll be fine. Just leave us here."

"You'll be fine?" She's had enough. "You can't just let him die here on the fucking beach! I know he's sick. We need to get help. You can't just let him bleed to death out here!"

Claude appears to return to consciousness. She walks over and stops Rae's frantic hands. "Why not?" she said. "It's what he wants. The hero here will be the person who does the least."

"It's what I want," Paul whispers in Rae's direction. "I don't need any help." He rests, eyes closing, and then finishes, "Let me die, Rae. I'm dying anyway." There is a minute or two of silence. And then, shocking them all, Paul begins to laugh. Weakly, but most definitely, with his eyes closed, he laughs.

Rae stands and wags her head in disbelief. This she has never seen. *This is insanity.* Doing nothing is against every impulse and work ethic she's honed in her professional life. But then she remembers the boosts in morphine, the yellow bands on thin, white wrists. She runs both her hands through her hair, blood on blonde, streaking it into a horrific mass. *Shit,* she thinks, *I didn't even have gloves on, and for all I know, this guy has AIDS.*

Rae's thoughts return to Sonny. She cannot fathom his reason for doing this—and to have Six with him! She looks at Sloan, always peculiar, but now blubbering and staring at the top of Paul's head as she holds his cheek against her chest. Rae stands and swings her head around. She sees that Claude has decided to go for a swim and is stroking out to sea. This is all so incredibly bizarre that maybe, just maybe, it makes some kind of sense, to someone if not to her.

"All right. All right then. But I'm not leaving. I won't touch you, but I am not leaving," she says to Paul.

She goes and sits away from the couple. Her mind floods with all the possible ramifications. Being the only rational person here, she will have to explain this to the hospital, to the *police.* She will somehow be accountable for this. She'll have to explain why this man was allowed to bleed to death here on the beach! *Why, why, why did Sonny do this?* Of all the men worthy of this act of retribution, why this innocent one?

She brings her hands in front of her eyes and stares at them as if they were not her own. *He is obviously very sick and, well, maybe gone is gone and it makes no difference which road you take out of town.*

Then she says, more to herself than anyone else, "We'll think of something." And with that she props her arms behind her, leans back, and allows nature to take its course.

Beneath the September sun and beyond the sun itself, all of God's creations witness another death as they witness a birth, with dread and then amazement. At the thought of death, our emotions become bulky and tied together with weak string. Some are vague, vapid feelings, and some are as intense as the sun's shards chucked into our eyes. So we close our eyes or get wasted or, in any way possible, hide. It is just too much, too big, this dying.

But there comes at death a transformation, which we acknowledge or do not. We might become the tip of a gull's wing or the crying of a child. We might be an angel always in the presence of the Divine. We might regroup into fluffs of clouds in the sky or garbage illegally dumped at sea or Sunday dinner with the in-laws. We might be the in-laws. It will still be you, but you reconfigured. You without remembering the other you, except for weird flashes of remembering. It is divine recycling, and time, or what passes as time, will pass regardless of whom or what we will have become.

Paul's elegant brown face is tight against the pale comfort of his wife's breast. The repetitive rising and falling as she breathes is slightly nauseating to him. He feels a dizzy lightness and a detachment from his body as precise as the leaving of a room. The amplified sound of his own breathing echoes in his head over and over—the sucking in as a hollow slurp, then the noisy exhalation.

He senses traveling in all directions at once, boundless expansion and implosion. None of this is frightening to him. He feels like a bystander.

He is again aware of her. *Her.* That very clear sense of *her.* The comfort and familiarity of *her.* The leaving and staying of *her.*

But now he is moving away. Away from her and her crying and her need. The wind is full of song and he is part of the singing. It vibrates within his body and this pleases him.

Though his eyes are closed, he witnesses the mess of color around him, the intense light of the risen sun, the lingering reds, oranges, and golds. He touches the blue of the sea with his memory.

He laughs at his predicament. He laughs at what he thought it would be like. He laughs, but does not feel the effects of laughter in his body. There is no sound, no change in breathing, no rattling or shaking or tears. Still it lingers, this silent, rapturous laughter. Again, the feeling of being a bystander.

He is now forgetting the details of his life. They are being washed together with his organs out to sea, just as he had wished. The waters will cleanse away every sin, every symptom of disease, every tear, all the loving things he did, all the lies.

As the blood flows from him he has the sense of being a radio, one with weak batteries, slowly losing power. The music of the wind is fading to a pleasant static. Then no more words are spoken in his head. And with his final breaths, Paul, the poet, the lover, the restaurateur, this man returns home once again.

TO FEED THE MUSTARD GREENS

DO NOT IGNORE THIS ONE THING, BELOVED,
THAT ONE DAY WITH THE LORD IS LIKE A THOUSAND YEARS,
AND A THOUSAND YEARS ARE LIKE ONE DAY.

2 Peter 3:8

In a kitchen that always smells of food, where the fragrances of last night's chicken mingle with the morning's bacon and coffee, in that bright, yellow kitchen stands a boy of seven years.

It is early morning. He has slept only in spurts the night before, waking again and again with the dread of what he now must do.

Exhaustion heightens his sensual awareness. The coffee smells like the charred remains of a trash fire. The sunlight in the room is too much; he can barely see. The conversation in his head is soon drowned out by the quiet in the house. This quiet worries him. *Has she gone out? Will he have to carry this around with him all day?*

Then she is there, and he is at once happy and terrified to see her. She senses something, smells it on him, but says nothing. He senses her knowing. It's a lesson, he figures, this making it hard on him, making him come to her. He sits at the table and stares at his cereal bowl. She pours the milk. Even one mouthful of food and he knows that he will surely throw up.

She walks about the kitchen, straightening, fussing at the stove, humming. She is waiting for him but pretends not to be.

He wants to tell her, but can't find the way to begin. Maybe he should stand — he might seem taller, older, less afraid. But his legs don't seem to be responding when he orders them to upright him. They are rubbery and trembling slightly, like a baby bird he once had held in his hands.

"Emmie," he says so softly it takes his grandmother a moment to realize he's spoken. "Emmie, I lost my bike," he blurts out, hoping she can figure out the rest and it will be done with. It's not just the loss of his bike, his for only eight days now. The way he lost it is the problem.

She is not aroused by this pronouncement, but wipes her hands on her apron, that perfect, pretty apron. She turns off a burner and stands above him, watching him, ready to listen.

He hopes she is not angry. She's been known to strike him, but not often. She does it when it's called for, not out of uncontrolled emotion. It could be delivered alongside the head, or hard enough on the bottom to drive him forward two or three steps before falling.

If he could hold back the tears, he would. But he can't, and they come streaming down his cheeks. They are no comfort to him and he knows they will not soften her. It's hard to talk because his breathing is so ragged, but he says to her, "They knocked me off it and took it. There was three of 'em."

He is too embarrassed to say more, to tell her how they had questioned him. "You want us to have your bike, right? We ain't stealin' it, right? Say it, you creepy little brown turd!"

He is only seven, but he had realized one thing as he sat there in the dirt looking at these three boys—older, bigger, mean boys. He could lose his bike and get beaten up bad, or he could just lose his bike.

"Take it," he told them. "Just take it!" he screamed. And then he got up and ran away from them and away from his beautiful, twenty-inch, glossy red Schwinn. As he ran, he hollered back at them, "I hate you! I hate you!" Over and over he said this. He never cried in front of them, of that and only that he is proud. Through that restraint, he had learned that anger can mask almost any other feeling. When you're angry, that is going to be all you feel.

This would also be true for Emmie. He knew she would be angry about the bike. It hadn't come easy; things had to be gone without.

Emmie does dearly love her grandson. He has always lived in her house; and she has raised him since his mother was killed when a kid in his father's truck jumped a curb on Woodward Avenue. The boy was only three then. Since the accident, his father, Emmie's own son, who had never been much of a parent, wasn't around much. He worked third shift at the plant, disappeared into sleep and bars much of the rest of the time. Never got over the loss of his wife, a lovely Haitian woman twenty-five years his junior.

"There mus' be mo' to it," she says to the boy now. It seems to her that everything comes so hard and leaves so easy.

Then she draws close and lowers herself onto her fleshy knees. She's eye to eye with the boy. She's so close, he can't help but look straight into her watery, ancient eyes. He sees the darker rings of blackness that circle them. He sees the pores in her skin and the tight gray curls along her hairline.

"I don't know 'em, Gramma. I don't think they're from around here."

"Was they white?"

"Ah huh." He begins to whimper again.

"Maybe they rich or as poor as you, no matter. Such a mean and hateful thing. Why do we treat each other this way?" Her eyes go up into her head. He guesses she is looking for some answers or maybe just coming up with his punishment. But then she brings her hands tight around his shoulders and pulls him closer yet. He is overcome with those aromas that for his lifetime will bring her to mind…the pure, almost scentless Miller's soap, the Wildroot, the smokey trail of bacon, the hint of the cherry-flavored cigars she sometimes favors in her room at night.

And then she delivers that one sentence that he will never, ever forget.

"Boy, if'n you can't find forgiveness at home, then where'll you gonna?"

He throws himself into her. He cries hard with his whole body. Emmie swallows up his suffering, makes it all right somehow, takes it into her and releases it like a bullet passing through.

"What'ya doin' up?" he hears her say.

"What's wrong with the boy?" It is the hard, accusing voice of his father, a figure so dark in the sunny kitchen he is a mere silhouette.

"Ain't nothin' wrong wit' him. Jus' too sweet for this world, that's all."

She had never told the boy that right after he was born, she had buried his placenta in her backyard beneath the mustard greens. Throughout that summer, she had laid over it coffee grounds and egg shells, and powerful incantations to her ancestors and the God deep within her. With these rituals and her daily acts of common love, she tied the boy to her with a knot so secure not even eternity would ever shake it loose.

ANOTHER KITCHEN, ANOTHER TIME

"Tell me why. If you don't tell me I won't know the next thing to do."
Sonny is on his knees and has the child propped up against the
kitchen cupboards. Her body is still limp and her eyes are nearly closed.

She says nothing, but he sees thin lines of liquid cupping in her lower
eyelids. "Talk to me, Six."

He lets her slide down to a sitting position on the floor. Her head
drops and her shoulders stiffen. He thinks she will break down then,
will sob and throw herself into his arms. But she does not. She brings
her face to meet his and there is a cold defiance and maturity in it that
is not her own, or at least not as he knows her.

This other child frightens him. He stands and picks up the rifle. Rae
had been right about keeping it loaded and accessible.

"It's not right, it's not ever right, to take another's life," he says.
"There is no honor in it no matter the reason you did it. I know this
is against your God's laws, not to mention the laws of the state of
New York."

She continues to stare at her father.

Sonny loses patience, stoops, and takes the child by the shoulders. "I
don't want to lose you. I have to know how to protect you. Goddam
it, Six, this is crazy! Why did you shoot Paul?"

"I saved him," she yells. And then in an eerily calmer voice, "You heard
him. He was gonna kill himself. He gave up. God would not forgive
him for doing that. I saved him from hell."

Sonny's jaw drops and he pulls her to him. "And what about you?" he
exhales into her ear. "What does God think about you?"

"He will forgive me. I have time."

And then, as sure as all the sweet scents of youth—all the near odor-
less perspiration and the earthy musk and the slightest hint of salt
water—as sure as all those scents he loves saturate her skin, Sonny is
certain of what he will do for his daughter. There is no other option.

September 8

Dying is an act of great intimacy.

I was invited to watch, but I felt I was intruding. So then the swimming.

Back on shore he was still alive. From a short distance I watched his blood drain. Witnessed his life leaving him. Witnessed the small last sips of breath. They were like words whispered to himself. There was a finite number and I could almost count them down. Say there were 157 breaths left. Then 156. A cloud slips delicately over the sun. Then 155. A few grains of sand find his eyelashes. 154. With each exhalation, it seemed he released his time on earth, a day, maybe a moment or an entire year. 137 was his first great loss. 123 a night of lovemaking. 101 was a painful, hidden lie he never confessed but wanted to. 99 was the warm rush of the sea against his skin.

I imagine that somewhere below 10 was this past summer, which feels like a lifetime to me but not to him, I'm sure. Just a sad, inadequate farewell.

When all his breaths were gone, I learned something else about death. With all the calamity and violence and the sharp cold of the water against my skin, with all the bizarre visuals in the way his death was delivered, it just didn't affect me the way I thought it would. I didn't expect the calm that followed.

There was this brief feeling of lightness, an airy joyfulness, that crept into me at the time he stopped breathing and lay there motionless in the early sun, his body ashine and empty. We were all silent, attentive to the sounds we had not been listening to. Loud slaps of water and shrieking gulls. Rae said she'd go for help. That seemed odd since Paul was now dead, so I assumed she meant help for herself and her family. Sloan, too, just stood up, expressionless, and walked away, back towards their cottage. Still shirtless and covered in his blood.

She was as I have come to know her over this summer. Beautiful, silent, lost.

I stayed with the body. Thought about the many questions that would be asked. I realized that there would be as many different answers as there were witnesses. How could any of us explain the misdirected heroism of a certain nine-year-old? I couldn't, so I just denied even being there when they asked what had happened. Judas unto the end. I'd simply found another body as I had earlier in the summer. He might as well have been Mr. Wretz. But when the police asked if I knew him, this time I had to admit that yes, I did, but only a little of him.

"Mr. Saugerties, we need to ask you some questions. I'm sorry, but they concern a delicate matter and we hope it doesn't offend you..."

"Get on with it."

"Yes, well, do you have any knowledge of a romantic...possibly sexual... relationship between your neighbor Rae Gutierrez and the recently deceased Paul Lang?"

"She's a whore. She sleeps with everybody. I saw them underneath her trailer, going at it like a couple of dogs."

"Okay. But, how did you know it was Mr. Lang? I mean, wasn't it dark?"

"I can see a nigger even in the dark..."

"Mr. Saugerties..."

"I heard the gunshot. Was far off, but I heard it. Woke me up. I knew it was a gunshot. Was in the service, you know."

"The gunshot yesterday? What time did you hear that?"

"The sun was up. Well, not up. It's the earth that rotates."

"Yes. Right. Uh, did you see anybody around the Gutierrez trailer after the gunshot?"

"Yep. I saw her come running down the lane there. She was calling for that mongrel of hers."

"You mean you saw Rae Gutierrez? Is that when she normally gets home from the hospital?"

"I don't know when she comes and goes. I ain't responsible for her. I ain't responsible for nothin'."

"And by mongrel, do you mean their pet? Do they have a pet?"

"Listen. I was doing what I was told to do."

"All right, then. Did you see Mr. Gutierrez at that time or any other time that day?"

"Yeah. He came back with the rifle in his hand."

"You sure of that?"

"I said it."

"Okay, then. Did he, did Mr. Gutierrez know about the incident, uh, under the trailer?"

"I heard him screaming at her. Called her a whore. Had every right to shoot that faggot. Had his honor to defend. I would of done the same if..."

"That faggot? You're saying that Mr. Lang was a homosexual? What makes you think that, Mr. Saugerties? Mr. Saugerties? Well, let's move on. You recently lost your wife, didn't you?"

"Nope. Don't know why you'd say that. She's in there...fixing my lunch, like she always does."

"Uh, okay. So that's your...your wife there, in the window?"

Cherry waves a leaf of lettuce at them, smiling. Then she lowers her head and calls out through the narrow window opening, "Just send him in when you're through with him, will you, boys?"

September 9

Another September morning, mild and bright, cloudless.

The whole thing feels like a dream. None of it in any logical order, a jumble of images and sounds.

If wakefulness can erase a dream in time, can a dream erase a mere few hours of remembering? Maybe.

Last night I dreamt about a sick child. Not someone I know, not Six, but a very young, very sick boy. I was holding him across my arms, explaining my concept of heaven to him, which I wish I could remember. I was not trying to cure him but to ease his fear. As I mumbled on, he became lighter and lighter, as if he would soon float upward. My words became a meaningless, but beautiful chant, and soon the boy jumped from my arms and ran away, laughing that wonderful silly chortle that children make when they get away cleanly. I woke up something close to happy. That hasn't happened in a long time.

Paul wasn't so much afraid of dying as of not dying well. I never helped him through any of it. I do feel honored to have witnessed his painful but poetic departure.

Sonny's confession is brave and creative and as believable as what actually happened.

I hear that Sloan is still stunned and speechless. I don't have the fortitude yet to go and see her. I will. Her silence now would be comfortable to be around. How strange.

September 23

To Six, when you are twenty-six, or fifty-six, or whenever,

If you find this journal in your hands, it means I felt you were ready to read my account of the summer you turned nine and changed the course of events for one eternal soul. Or maybe I have followed Paul, and in taking possession of the Airstream that I will have bequeathed to you, you've come across these yammerings of mine. Regardless, this will be my final entry into this journal.

This summer has been a collage of the ordinary and the alarming. My recounting of it is as fragmentary as my memory of each day's contents, even on the following day. What I have omitted far exceeds my personal obsessive ramblings. Forgive me. My only hope is that through these words, you will glimpse the bravery and decency you exhibited. It far surpassed all our efforts.

If these three months had been a play, my role would be the most minor. I was required to be convincing in my passion, but the anguish and obsession were all my own. Perhaps, now, you as an adult can understand my greed and transformation. Sex can lead you to love, but it's not always the love you imagined. Forgive my indulgences and the graphic details of my encounters with Sloan. All that she asks of me now is that I randomly read Paul's poems to her. They are kept in a cardboard box on the mantelpiece, right next to the cardboard box containing Paul's ashes. And maybe this will be the last act in our play, with me reading to the two of you.

There were betrayals in our drama, performed out in the open air, making them less betrayal than collusion. Even your mother's infidelities and shortcomings (I hope you don't judge her too harshly) were the result of lack of preparation on her part for the roles of wife and mother.

Our play was also riddled with crimes. There was a planned suicide and, as you well know, an actual felony, and many fabrications and acts of deception. But because the motivations for many of the offenses were honorable, I believe they were crimes not against humanity, but rather, in its defense. Your father is in jail and making up answers to so many questions. There is no greater act of love than his sacrifice for you.

Rae told me the police are suspicious. Even with a confession in hand, they are still looking for reliable witnesses and a logical scenario. Problematic is the delay between the time of the shooting and its being reported in a 911 call by me. They know the wound did not inflict major organ damage, and they keep asking why it took so long for people to respond. I claimed I just came upon the body during my routine morning beach walk. Rae claimed she was already dead asleep and never heard the gunshot or noticed that her husband was missing. Nobody has thought to talk to you.

Also baffling are the autopsy results and the hospital medical records that indicate Paul's advanced disease. His alleged affair with your mother was difficult for them to believe, but again, there was a witness. Saugerties had been no friend to you until, in his deep confusion, he found the lies and enough sanity and humanity to protect you. Or maybe it was Cherry who coached him in the sweet deception.

Even more odd is your mother's devotion to your father. She misses him greatly, says so often, and even tends his garden, cares for the chickens.

But there is a sense of waiting for something to happen in the air, maybe the true arrival of autumn, not the calendar event, but the consistent coolness, the darker days, the pungent fragrance of must. The leaves are already looking fatigued and heavy, anxious to fall.

We all wait for time and the seasons to hurry and blur one into the next, as they will so predictably do. There is some comfort in that.

Twelve days ago, Six, the world fell apart. You and I looked west from the beach, across the body of land that is Long Island to the graveyard that lower Manhattan had become. It was that perfect June day replicated in September, a beautiful, beautiful day gone up in smoke and ash and paper snowflakes. It was still beautiful in East Marion and impossible for us to believe the chaos unfolding only a hundred miles away. The collapse of those two buildings dwarfed our loss and made it seem like the whole world was grieving. I fear that our retaliation will take more innocent lives. What changes will this bring in the world and in us?

But there is always great beauty in this world, Six, and I know you are sensitive to this. I have seen every grain of sand on fire with the glorious colors of an ordinary sunset here. I have seen the color of your skin change over the summer into the most luxurious bronze imaginable, a color that reflects your lineage and love of the natural world. Look into your own eyes right now and tell me you don't see what I saw, because there is a world of determination and beauty and depth in those eyes that I cannot possibly describe here.

During this past summer here in our own little world, there was beauty and loss, too, but also great acts of love. Those are what I hope you remember.

I imagine that, by the time you read this, you will have made your own way. I can picture you as an artist or a preacher. A mother. I hope I still know you.

Claude